DRUGSTORE
COWBOY

DRUGSTORE
COWBOY
James Fogle

DELTA FICTION

A Delta Book
Published by Dell Publishing
a division of
Bantam Doubleday Dell Publishing Group, Inc.
666 Fifth Avenue
New York, New York 10103

The trademark Delta® is registered
in the U.S. Patent and Trademark Office.

Library of Congress Cataloging in Publication Data

Fogle, James.
    Drugstore cowboy / by James Fogle.
        p.   cm.
    ISBN 0-385-30224-1
    I. Title.
    PS3556.O35D78   1990
    813'.54—dc20   90-32939   CIP

Designed by GDS / Jeffrey L. Ward

Published simultaneously in Canada

To all the poor junkies who fell around me that summer of 1974 and to the light of my love, Maybelle Lincoln, and my old pards, Jack Reardon, Red Robby, Pat Hammond, Don Soames, and Bobby Emmet, who all died either that summer or shortly afterward in connection with the use and traffic of drugs.

PART I

Bob was lying in the back seat of the car, thinking of all the ways to rip off drugstores. He had done them all, with the pharmacies open or closed; it didn't matter, except for technique. A lot of Bob's work was sheer inspiration. You didn't read about it in any crime novel or see it on those television police shows. No, it was too good for that, too personal. Bob figured he was qualified to write a book, if he could ever sit down long enough in one place to do it. It would be titled *A Dope Fiend's Guide to Drugstores,* or something like that. And in it the curious reader would find flights of fancy, gems of creativity, artistry, and yes, even honest-to-goodness poetry.

Of course, Bob had also done a lot of the standard stuff, like picking locks or sawing holes in roofs. Yeah, sawing holes; Bob liked to do that. When working away in his fast and efficient way with hand drills and saws and such, he even thought of himself as a half-assed carpenter.

Bob giggled out loud as he thought of a conversation he had gotten into with a pharmacist at his mother's house one night. Here his mom was keeping a sharp eye on him, ready to slap him down for any funny stuff he might think to pull in front of her friend and invited guest, and of course the guy had no idea that right there in that living room, in the person of that sweet woman's agreeable-looking son, was one of the cleverest and ringiest and most notorious dope-fiend drugstore cowboys on the entire West Coast, including Alaska.

So here was Bob, sympathizing with the poor man's tale of woe and pretending that he didn't know what the guy was talking about as he rattled off all those technical names for this or that drug. And the man was saying, "Yeah, I got hit a few times in the old store, but it hasn't happened here yet. We had a flat roof in the old building and they used to saw right down through the roof, can you believe it?" And Bob could hardly contain himself, even with his mom staring him down, 'cause it was not at all unlikely that the madman with the saw at the old store on one of those dark, foggy West Coast nights was none other than Bob, this sweet mother's son, right here himself.

Bob giggled some more and yelled out, "Yeah, I think we'll give it the old beaver shot this time."

Up in the front seat, his partners knew he wasn't expecting a response. They had grown used to Bob being in his own world back there, giggling to himself, relaxing and possibly psyching himself up for the work ahead. They didn't bother him at moments like this, because they knew he was ringy and they also knew he was good, and they knew that if he was feeling that everything was going their way, well, then they could feel that way too.

The car pulled over and stopped. Bob got out first and casually walked down the sidewalk as if he were appreciating the weather or thinking about buying a toy for a son or daughter. With his gray corduroy trousers and nondescript sport shirt, with his short cropped and neatly groomed light-brown hair, Bob looked like everything but what he was.

An old woman with a white poodle on a leash approached. "Nice day, huh?" Bob beamed in passing. His smile was quite pleasant and hid the time he had spent in reform schools, correctional institutions, and penitentiaries. His clear blue eyes, unlined face, and white teeth said nothing of the many years he had injected narcotics into his bloodstream. His quiet demeanor belied the stimulant runs of the past.

Bob was a walking paradox as he strolled down the sun-drenched sidewalk in the downtown section of Portland, Oregon, and turned into a pharmacy. He walked by the checkout counter, passed in front of the pharmacist's counter, and took up his post in front of the veterinary supplies, looking over the items on display.

The next person to enter the store was a woman. Like Bob, she looked neither young nor old. She wasn't especially pretty, but she made up for it with careful attention to her long, dark-brown hair. Her clothes were her best asset; they exuded expensive, fashion-conscious tastes. In Bob's words, "All decked out like that she looked like

an everyday, homey old haybag with a little bread."
Which was exactly the impression she hoped to convey.

But Diane was far from that. She was a dope fiend of
the first degree, with a past like something out of *Ripley's
Believe It or Not.* She may have once been homey, since
she did have three children, though she hardly ever saw
them anymore and her thoughts of motherhood were
almost as rare as her visits.

Diane had been known to get what she was after simply
by grabbing it out of a pharmacist's hands and running
like hell, or by waving a gun in the man's face and demanding the drugs as if the guy were maliciously trying
to keep her from what was rightfully hers. She had stuck
it out on roofs in the freezing rain as her partner sawed
his way into pharmacy sections. And she had not hesitated to put the make on some poor unsuspecting doctor
to achieve her ends. Diane was an all-around girl, and in
Bob's eyes, daily proved her worth with her intelligence
and cool professionalism.

The next person to enter the pharmacy was a blond
girl not long out of her teens. Her blouse was scanty and
her skirt stopped well short of her knees. She had all the
right bulges in all the right places. She was the only one
of the group who looked exactly like what she was, a
young, dumb broad.

Nadine had no record. She was just beginning the
lifestyle that would eventually lead to her death.

The fourth member of the gang was Rick. He was the
muscle. Since he was just beginning his career with Bob
and Diane, he was an unproved subject to them, and
would remain just that until he fell, held tough, and later
rejoined their company. But he was no novice to the life

of crime. His record indicated a steady climb from juvenile offender to small-time thief.

Nadine proceeded down the store's main aisle and stopped at the perfume counter. Rick took up his post near the entrance, pretending to look through the get-well cards. Meanwhile, Diane was engaged in an over-the-counter conversation with the druggist. She initially had caught him off guard with a highly irrational question, and was progressively exasperating him with irrelevancies and incomprehensible interjections.

Bob gave the signal, Diane passed it along by scratching her rear, and Nadine went into her act. She screamed and fell backward against a low display case, leaving her body arched to make the most of the fact that she wore nothing beneath her short skirt. She began to convulse and jerk, trying to mimic the symptoms of an epileptic seizure. Actually she looked more like some arched shimmy girl with no pants. Her blond, beaver-draped vagina plunged, leaped and lunged, seemingly screaming out for the spotlight.

The pharmacist immediately forgot about his problems with Diane and raced around the counter. He stopped several feet short of Nadine, however, confused by her apparent sickness and mesmerized by her exposed privates.

Bob made his move, quickly ducking behind the vacated counter and dropping to his knees. He scooted along, looking for any drawer or cabinet with a lock. Midway along the counter, he found what he was looking for. The large, cream-colored drawer was unlocked and slid out freely. Bob was about to raise his head high enough to look into it when he caught a flash of white out of the corner of his eye. He also heard Diane's cough, the signal that he might be in danger.

Bob slid quickly to the end of the counter and peered around the corner. He satisfied himself that the white flash had been the checkout girl, carrying something to cover Nadine's lower half, and scurried back to the drawer. Straightening up on his knees, he began rifling the contents of the drawer. It only took seconds, but it seemed like minutes to Bob. The sweat stood out on his forehead, neck, and chest. His hands started to shake and his knees quivered and jerked as he scooted back down the aisle, around the pill shelves, and into the back room, silently praying that the back door would open easily.

He heard Diane go through another fit of coughing. The pharmacist was no doubt on his way back to the counter to call an ambulance or something, Bob thought. Oh, well, this wouldn't be the first time he had to fight his way out of a pharmacy's back room.

He tried the back door. It was locked, with one of those antipick, antibudge, burglar-proof locks, the kind with three metal rings that all line up, with a solid pin holding them together until the key raises the pin, enabling the center ring to swing out of position as the door opens. Bob took this in at a glance, then looked at the hinges. He assumed they would be the lock-in type and was pleasantly surprised to see that they weren't. They were the simple kind with only a knob on one end.

Bob quickly placed a screwdriver between the knob of the hinge pin and the top of the hinge and pried upward. One, two, three, the hinges slipped out easily, like greased pigs. Of course, the door now looked a little funny, kind of out of kilter, with lots of daylight showing around the unmatched edges.

But Bob didn't care, he was home free. He walked casually away, down the alley to the car, which was parked around the corner on the next block. Never run, that was one of Bob and Diane's basic rules. No matter what happens, don't panic. And never run.

Back in the drugstore, Diane, who had coughed herself hoarse, asked if they weren't too busy to take her money for a bottle of cough syrup, smiled for the benefit of all, and quietly left the premises. Nadine, who had stopped jerking about by now, remained arched over the display case, feigning exhaustion to give Diane a little lead time in her departure. An ambulance siren sent a chill up her spine, however; so she sat up, quickly rearranged her clothing and hair, tried without much success to appear embarrassed, deftly disengaged the hands holding her, and walked out the door. She was followed by Rick, still grinning, who had remained by the card rack, chuckling through the whole show.

The pharmacist and the checkout girl looked on in amazement as they left. To the girl, it was a phenomenal event, the likes of which she had never seen before. But it didn't actually occur to her that something might be wrong. In the pharmacist's thoughts, however, was the nagging suspicion that he had been had. He later told the narcotics officers, "But it all happened so fast!"

When Diane entered the auto, Bob was lying low in the back seat, feigning sleep. She immediately asked, "How'd we do?"

Bob grinned and shrugged his shoulders, as much as he could from his reclined position. "So-so," he said.

Diane started the engine and nervously sat tapping the steering wheel with her long, tapered fingernails. "I wish them two would get a move on. I've told them and told them to get the fuck out once we've made our move."

Bob raised up enough to look out the back window. "For chrissakes, Diane, watch your fucking language. Who in hell do you think you are, Ma Barker or something?"

Diane turned in the front seat and spat out, "Just who in the fuck do you think you are, my father? If you can cuss, so can I, goddamnit!"

Bob sat up and kept looking out the rear window until he spotted them. Rick and Nadine were casually strolling down the sidewalk, hand in hand, toward the car. Bob opened the door and called out, "Come on, come on, I said walk, not crawl!"

As they took their places in the front seat next to Diane, Nadine, her back to Bob, said in her little-girl, nasty manner, "You said walk and that's what we done, walk. Can't we do nothing right?"

"Yeah, I said walk, but I didn't mean you had to window-shop all along the way."

Rick just grinned as though nothing more was expected of him. And nothing was.

As soon as Diane had driven a few blocks and was in the midst of downtown traffic, Bob called out from the back seat, "Anybody got an outfit up there?"

Diane turned, completely disregarding the traffic. "Goddamnit, Bob, what you got to fix in the car for? Can't you wait until we get home like everybody else?"

Bob grinned at her and said, "Shut up and watch your driving."

He didn't want to fix in the car. He hated fixing in moving vehicles. He just wanted to start something, because he had nothing to do and was getting bored and restless lying back there all by himself.

But the talk of a fix suddenly reminded Bob of the drugs in his possession. He scratched his head as he realized they had gone perhaps a quarter of a mile without his thoughts once turning to the object of their little business excursion. Jesus, he could hardly believe it! But now the rest of the world faded away as he settled back and let the good feelings flow.

He felt the exhilaration of having just pulled off another fair score; of having formulated a plan, put it in motion, and watched it get results. And then, of course, there was the anticipation of an impending big fix. There was just no describing how good that felt. To have the goods in hand and know that in a few minutes . . . nothing could compare to a feeling like that, unless, of course, it was the actual experience itself.

After any kind of drug haul, everyone in the crew indulged to the utmost. Bob laughed to himself as he pictured blues or Dilaudid in such great amounts that the spoon would literally be overflowing. Upon entering his vein the drug would start a warm itch that would surge along until it hit the brain in a gentle explosion that began in the back of the neck and rose rapidly, until he felt such pleasure that the whole world took on a soft, lofty appeal. Everything was grand then. Your worst enemy—he wasn't so bad. The ants in the grass—they were just doing their thing. Everything took on the rosy hue of unlimited success; you could do no wrong; life was beautiful.

Then as soon as the flash of the heavy narcotics was gone, he and the others would switch to stimulants, and again they would cook up as much as their spoons and outfits would hold. This time the reaction was different, burning up the arms and the back of the neck, literally standing their hair on end, before settling in the mouth. And no matter how bad the solution tasted in a spoon, it was always mildly pleasant to the taste buds after it had passed into the bloodstream. At the same time, a warm feeling of well-being gradually increased, accompanied by a pounding pulse and small pleasure tremors streaking off in different directions (usually down the legs after starting in the pelvic region), until hair, skin, and clothes were literally sweat-soaked with the joy of it all.

When this wore off, it was back to the heavy stuff— Dilaudid, Numorphan, or morphine. If the drugs held out, one could spend his entire life hung up in a bathroom or kitchen switching back and forth, Bob mused. He himself had done exactly that for days on end, shooting as much as he thought he could get away with without actually killing himself.

Up in the front seat, Diane fought the traffic and swore like a trooper. A few choice four-letter words drifted into Bob's consciousness and broke his concentration. He switched his attention to Diane, and playfully began berating her about her foul mouth, and what the hell kind of example was she setting for the youngsters, anyway? And so Diane came right back at him, claiming that he was goddamn lucky that she had to keep her eyes on the road and the steering wheel in her hands, because otherwise he probably would have been a candidate for strangling.

Whereupon Bob reminded her to keep her eyes on the road and her hands on the steering wheel, because it didn't look to him that she was doing a very good job of it, and it was his life that she was responsible for.

Nadine sat in silence. It just didn't do to be outspoken around these people. They thought they knew so goddamn much, and perhaps they did, since they seemed to do just about anything they wanted to and somehow get away with it. One thing was for damn sure, they knew how to make money and get narcotics.

Rick was also quiet. He knew from experience not to get into it when Bob and Diane were carrying on, because if he chose to agree with one of them, they would immediately team up and jump on him. It was the way things went. If there were two things Diane and Bob liked to do, it was hassle people and shoot dope. Rick often wondered which of the two they liked the most.

On the other side of town, Diane pulled up in front of their apartment. She unlocked the front door and immediately went to the bedroom, returning to the living room with a small leather cigar case in her shaking hands. Rick splintered off to the kitchen to get spoons and a glass of water. He left Nadine standing in the middle of the living room, sniffing with quiet disdain that anyone or any group of people could be in so much of a hurry to stick a damn needle in their arm.

Bob was sitting on the couch with his leather belt beside him. He rummaged through his pockets and pulled out bottle after bottle, all of them fairly small, some only a fraction of an inch long and three quarters of an inch in diameter. Every time he found another and laid it on the coffee table in front of him, Diane let out a small, sibilant gasp that was almost sexual in its expectation of more, more, more.

By now Bob was gasping himself. It seemed to be catching, because Rick also joined in, picking up the rhythm.

Nadine looked on in disgust. How could anyone get so excited over a few small bottles? They might be worth a lot of money, but she wouldn't see any of it. The bottles would be empty in a matter of days. Between the three of them, Bob, Diane, and Rick could shoot up fifteen hundred dollars' worth of dope a day. Nadine had often watched them do it, even though she had only been with the group a little more than a month.

Diane spoke first. "Didn't you get no blues?"

Bob flashed his practiced evil grin, reached into a rear pocket, and placed two slightly larger brown bottles in front of Diane. It was the same old ritual, Nadine thought as she watched Diane clasp her hands and gasp in a climax that stirred everyone in the room.

Then everyone got down to business, even Nadine. After all, if she had to go through all the crap, she might as well reap some of the benefits, even if it did still send her to the toilet bowl with a howling stomach. She often wondered if her stomach would ever get used to the idea. She supposed it would, eventually, because none of the others seemed to be bothered. The damn smartasses, every time she asked when she would get over her stomach troubles, all they would do was laugh and say, hang on to it, baby, you'll wish you could get back that queasy stomach a thousand times before you're through. Well, maybe so, Nadine thought, but right now she just wished her stomach would smooth out a little. It seemed like she held almost nothing down there anymore.

As everyone grabbed a spoon, Diane took the one-c.c. syringe out of the small leather cigar case. They were cut off, with the plunger pulled and a baby pacifier stretched over the large end. They were more practical than a medical syringe from an addict's point of view, primarily because they were easier to use with one hand. Also the register—the initial bubble or small intake of blood signaling the needle's entry into the wall of the vein—was almost automatic. All you had to do was tie off and poke around, watching the clear bottom of the syringe. When you spotted the blood, you squeezed the pacifier, displacing the air and pushing the liquid in the syringe through the needle and into the vein. It was as simple as that, if you had a vein left to poke into, that is. Diane didn't. Bob only had a few to dicker with. Sometimes they'd do the job and sometimes they wouldn't. Rick had no trouble at all. And as for Nadine, she was virtually a virgin in this department. Bob often claimed he could hit her just by throwing the outfit, as if he were horsing around with darts or something.

Diane was more or less the queen of the group, and always got first consideration when anything was being fixed. So Bob looked to her first. "How much you want, babe?"

Diane hemmed and hawed and finally said, "Oh, I don't know, give me a blue and a couple sixteenths."

Bob frowned. "You think you can handle all that?"

"You damn right!"

"Okay, babe," Bob shrugged. "Here you go."

He handed her a ten milligram Numorphan tablet. It was blue and about the size and consistency of an aspirin. It was also a powerful narcotic, possibly the most powerful known to man. Ten milligrams taken intravenously or intramuscularly would in most cases be considered a lethal dose. Taken along with two sixteenths of Dilaudid in the form of two very small white pills, this dose would undoubtedly kill anyone but a confirmed addict. A sixteenth of Dilaudid is comparable to a dose of heroin or a half grain of morphine.

Diane clutched the pills, staring at them in wonder. Then she carefully placed them in her spoon. "You're going to help me?" she asked Bob.

Bob nodded and looked to Rick.

"Give me a blue." Rick grinned.

Bob turned to Nadine. She shrugged. "Give me the same, I guess."

Bob smiled. "No, I don't think so, Nadine."

"Why not?" she whined.

Diane brought her head up and looked right through Nadine, scoffing, "Nadine, you can't shoot no goddamn blue. Give her half of one, Bob, that'll keep her in the crapper all afternoon."

Nadine fought back. "Goddamnit, I was in there just like you. I ought to get the same as everyone else, even if I can't shoot it all right now. I could save it, or maybe sell it and get me a few things."

Bob turned serious, and after thinking a moment said, "Well, Nadine, I'll tell you what. That just ain't the way things work around here. You ain't worth all that much to begin with. All you've done is shag your twat, and that ain't nothing. I can get a dozen bitches to do that and be happy to get the goddamn chance. It's me that's taking the big risk. If we get busted, there's nothing they can do to you. What are they going to try you for, having a fit in a drugstore? Hell no, they ain't, they're going to piss and moan a little and cut you loose—that is, if you've got sense enough to keep your mouth shut."

"Well, how about Diane? She ain't done nothing either. All she did was stand around and cough. She didn't have to show her damn ass to everyone in town."

Bob sat back in the couch. "Okay, Nadine," he sighed. "What do you want, a fourth of everything I got?"

Diane, who was injecting the dark-blue liquid into a vein in her hand, looked up long enough to say, "Don't give her a goddamn thing. Kick her ass out in the street, where we found her."

"No, no, fair is fair," Bob said, shaking his head. "You want your fourth, you got it, Nadine. But I ain't taking on no apprentices and giving them a full end of my thing. You take it and get out!"

At this, Nadine looked confused. She held out her hand, but she wasn't sure if she should, and she was beginning to realize that she didn't know what she wanted.

Rick, who had just fixed in the ditch of his arm—straight up—grimaced and barked, "Goddamn you, Nadine! Take your half blue, shut up, shoot it, and go puke awhile!"

Nadine slowly withdrew her hand and turned away from everyone. Bob laid the half tablet on the edge of the coffee table near her and began his own thing, which would top them all. He took out a blue and four six-teenths.

Bob was in the middle of fixing when they heard a knock on the door. He gave Diane a quick nod and she deftly scooped up all the bottles and ran for the bed-room. Bob quickly untied the belt on his arm, secured it around his waist, and drew a .45 caliber automatic pistol from under a couch cushion. Holding it at arm's length, pointed at the floor, he approached the door's peekhole.

He recognized the knocker. It was David, one of the least honorable street kids from the downtown area. There was a whole clique of those raggedy little mon-sters. You could usually find them, or at least one of them, somewhere around the bus depot. They earned their living by stealing personal articles off transient pas-sengers or by selling sex to the many servicemen that passed through the bus station. They had no honor at all; they were capable of anything. Bob demanded, "What do you want, David?"

"I just want to see you for a minute, Bob. Let me in."

"You alone?"

"Hell, yes, I'm alone. What'd you think, I brought my rat-faced granny along to hold my hand?"

Bob nodded to Rick and Nadine, who were standing as though stuck to the floor. They didn't move, so he stepped back from the door and commanded in a whisper, "You, Nadine, pick up those spoons, outfits, and that glass of water. Rick, get your goddamn gun out and get in the bedroom and back me up."

Both Nadine and Rick jumped at his orders. Bob had so quickly changed his whole demeanor; now he was intent, alert. The laugh lines around his eyes had quickly faded away, and his dilated, dark pupils had become like hard, glass marbles. Bob seemed so spooky that he gave Nadine the shivers.

But Bob was like that whenever he held anything worthwhile. "What the hell," he'd say to Diane. "Between the damn narco bulls and the rip-off artists, one can't be too goddamned careful."

You really never knew which it would be, Bob knew, until they hit you. Then it was too late. You were either in jail, sick as a dog and fighting another case, or you were lying on the floor of your own apartment with a paper sack over your head, your ribs kicked in, your old lady raped a couple of times, and all your hard-earned dope gone. In fact, at that point, if they didn't just casually pump a couple of bullets in you, you considered yourself lucky as hell.

And for some damn reason, every dope fiend in the area could tell if you were holding. It didn't make any difference how careful you were. They could sense it, they could almost smell it—the hangers-on, the rip-off artists, that is. Not the cops. They couldn't smell a dead rat two feet away. But the damn dope-fiend snitches could. They could tell just by the way you drove in the yard, by the way you hurried into the apartment, and if you made a studied, careful approach, they could sense it even more. There was just no way to improvise that disgusted, sick feeling of coming home with nothing. In fact, Bob refused to come home empty-handed. He'd run his heart out first, and then come home and lay in agony for days on end before someone gave him a throw out or until he became well enough to get out and go back to work; and everyone knew it.

Bob opened the door and pointed his cocked gun at the long-haired, grubby, disheveled young man who stood there. David's hair was a dirty-looking burnt red and hung down to almost hide his rodentlike features, his small, pointed face and long nose.

It was his always alert, small, shifting eyes that showed him for what he was, though: a smallish, clever, and cruel youth who always seemed to have a pleasant smile pasted on his street-weary face. David backed up a step and then asked, "What the hell, pard, you finally gone completely crazy or something?"

It was an act they had played several times before, but Bob never relaxed his vigil. That way, the sonsofbitches knew when they crashed his pad, they'd have to crash it shooting. Most dope fiends didn't have the heart for that. And if they did, Bob hoped at least to keep them off balance.

David smiled at the ritual. He slowly stepped into the apartment and looked over Bob's shoulder to see Rick's arm and gun protruding around the doorjamb of the bedroom. Then he carefully took off his jacket, swirled around like a ballet dancer doing his swan number, and relaxed as Bob lowered his pistol and thumbed the hammer from full to half cock.

David also smiled because he knew Bob was holding. Bob would never go through the complete ritual unless he was holding big or trying to impress someone.

David flopped on the couch and settled into a half sitting, half lying position. He looked around the room. Bob and Rick still held their pistols, but at arm's length now, pointed toward the floor. Nadine, clutching the sticky blue pill in her moist right hand, stood in the kitchen archway. David wondered where Diane was hiding. He guessed she had gone out the bedroom window to stash whatever they had in the shrubbery. Finally, he asked Bob outright, "What are you holding, pard?"

"I ain't holding shit, David," Bob answered, trying his best to look innocent. "I was just thinking of dropping by your place to see if you've got any speed."

David smiled. He knew he had Bob now. Bob was notorious for never buying any kind of dope with cash. Oh, he'd trade some of this for some of that, but put out actual bills for narcotics, never. He often claimed that he'd go without first, and eventually quit using if he ever had to bring himself to actually buy dope. Sometimes he did go without, too, just to prove his point, and at those times he nearly drove Diane up a tree. Her principles were not nearly as strict as Bob's. When she was sick she wanted dope, and she didn't care how she got it.

"Well, I got some speed," David said, with a somewhat embarrassed laugh.

Bob listened to David's admission and wondered if he really did want speed. When he decided he did, he tried to figure out just how much he should get. At this point his mind was more than a little foggy and figuring didn't come easily. Finally, he asked David, "What kind of speed you got?"

"Methedrine crystal."

Bob grinned. "You know what, David? You could have little balls of shit wrapped up in those little cellophane bags of yours, and I could ask you what you got, and your answer would always be the same, Methedrine crystal."

"No, Bob, really, this is good stuff—clears right up in

the spoon, no residue, hair-raising flash. Here, you try one on the house."

Bob responded with a look of pure skepticism. Then he asked, "Okay, how much you got on you right now?"

"Ten grams," David answered, without a moment's hesitation.

Bob looked to the bedroom. "Okay, just a moment. I got to talk to Diane first."

Bob entered the bedroom and found Diane straddling the windowsill, still clutching her armload of small bottles. She had not missed a word spoken in the other room, and now her face showed dissatisfaction with the way things were going and a strong doubt that Bob had her best interests at heart.

Bob just grinned at her sheepishly. "How about some speed, baby?" he asked. "The man says he's got Methedrine crystal."

Diane knew exactly what David had said, and what Bob's answer had been. She knew Bob well enough to imagine the look on his face and the thoughts on his mind even if silence had been the rule of negotiation. Her response was the same every time. "What do you want that goddamn speed for? You know how ringy it makes you. It turns you into a different person, Bob, and I don't much like that person."

Bob held out his hands, palms upward, as if to say, "Oh, what the hell, one more time isn't going to hurt anything, and I kind of like it. Give me a pass just this one last time and I'll be all right, I always am." And then his eyes took on a special kind of gleam. Diane called it his stealing gleam. An idea was forming in his mind that would work everything to his favor.

Diane watched as he finished sorting out his web of intrigue. Finally he spoke, his voice and features taking on the excitement of a small boy, ringing with confidence and the anticipation of a brand-new adventure. "Baby, listen to me, what night is it anyway? It's Saturday, right? How about us getting some speed, see, and then after we're all straightened out we'll all jump in the car and head down to Forty-fifth and get that big fat pharmacy, the one right next to the welfare office. I know we can do it, babe, I just been saving it for a hot Saturday night. You know how these things go, it's just like a crap game, right? When you're hot, you shoot the works, and when you're cold, you lay off a bit. Well, right now I'm hot, baby, I'm so hot I'm burning all over. I can feel it, I can see it, it's ours, Diane, it's ours, that goddamn drugstore is mine right now. I can feel it, it's right in my pocket, right this minute. It's mine."

Diane still straddled the windowsill; she hadn't budged an inch. She was moved—oh, the sonofabitch moved her all right—but she wasn't going to show it and she wasn't giving in that damn easy, either.

"All right, buster," she said. "If you're so goddamn hot, why don't you lay me down on the bed and make love to me right now?"

Bob turned away in disgust. "Oh, crap, you know what I mean, Diane. I'm hot to steal. We can fuck any god-damn time."

"Bullshit, you ain't fucked me in a month, what do you mean, we can fuck anytime? Why ain't we been fucking, then?"

Bob moved quickly and slammed the bedroom door. Turning back to Diane, he almost whispered out his plea,

"For chrissakes, you got to bring up crap like that at a time like this?"

He looked around as if trying to spot the answer to his problems. When his eyes settled on Diane again, his voice had firmed up. "So, okay, I ain't been doing so good in that department. What do you want me to do, go down the street and pick you up some young kid? I'm hooked, baby, I'm not like a woman. I can't just lay down and let some fool wear himself out trying to please me. I got to be the one that gets it up first and then has the energy to do all that. What do you expect me to do, you filthy female pervert, get down and lick it like a dog?"

Diane drew her outside leg back over the windowsill and into the room. "Shit," she began, sounding disgusted. "How much goddamn speed you going to get off that creep? Be sure and get me some, you sonofabitch. Lick it, my ass, you ain't got the sense God gave a pup, and don't you ever call me a filthy female pervert again or I'll cut your fucking heart out!"

Bob relaxed and grinned. "I know you will, baby, I know you would, and I'll be sure to get enough for all of us."

He returned to the living room and immediately began to dicker. "How much you asking for that crap anyway, David?"

"You know the going price, thirty bucks a gram," David grinned.

"All right. Give me five grams. I ain't got no money, but we can make a trade. What do you need?"

"You got any blues?"

Bob looked perplexed, almost amazed that such a question would be entertained, let alone asked. "Hell no,

I ain't got no blues! You know how hard it is to pick up blues these days?"

"How about Dilaudid, you got any sixteenths?"

Bob's eyebrows went up again. "Hell no, if I had six-teenths, you think I'd be sitting here rapping to you about some crappy speed? Hell no, I wouldn't. I wouldn't even have answered your knock. I'd be sitting here, right here in the middle of the fucking floor with a bitch on either arm. I'd just hold the ties and let them babies pump it in. You know that, David. You know how old Bob works. Now, how about some morphine? I got some good old morphine. And there ain't nothing better than good old pure morphine to take the edge off a man and pick his balls up out of the sand."

"What'd you get, man, morphine sulfate? Quarters or halves?"

Bob lapsed into black jargon himself when dealing with someone like David, although he hated it. "Yeah, man, I got quarters and halves. Of course, it's got a little atropine in it, but that won't hurt nothing. Just take you a little old ink blotter, lay the tablets out on it in rows, take a little old eyedropper, and place one drop of water on each one. Let them set a minute, no more, no less, and the atropine eases right off into the blotter and you're home free. Throw the little fellers off in the spoon and you're raring to go. Simple as falling off a sick whore."

David was visibly nervous. "Man, first I got to take the prickles of morphine and now you want to dehydrate me as well with atropine. You're crazy, man. I can't even read a stop sign when I'm on that crap, my eyes go so far out of focus. I ain't trading no uptown crank for no down-town trash."

"Well, you know how it is these days, David. It's a seller's market. I didn't come to your place begging no deal, you came here, stepped right in through this here fucking door, and said you had some Methedrine crystal to trade and what would I give you for it. And I told you, pard, I'll give you atropine morphine. That's all I got and all I can give, so what more can I say?"

"Bullshit, bullshit, bullshit. If you didn't have nothing more you wouldn't be even trading off that. You think I'm dumb, man, but I'm not as dumb as you think!"

Bob spread out his hands in front of him and shrugged. "Man, what can I say?"

David fussed and fumed, drew himself up on the couch, finally stood and made as though he was heading for the door.

Bob just grinned at him. "Too bad we couldn't do business, pard. Sorry I ain't got what you need. See you around. Maybe we can do some good for each other next time."

At the last minute, David turned away from the door, flung five packets of the white fluffy powder onto the coffee table, and asked, "Okay, man, how many quarter grains of atropine morphine you going to give me for that?"

Bob smiled, even though he knew he shouldn't. He turned to try to hide the emotions of triumph. "How about six quarters per package," he said finally, with a straight face. "Let me see, six times five, that would be twenty-eight, right?"

"Six quarters for a thirty dollar package? Man, that ain't no fucking deal, them packages is worth thirty bucks apiece. Where am I going to get five bucks apiece for them goofy quarters? Even if I burned somebody, I couldn't get no money like that. No, you trying to get me killed, that's what you're doing, you're trying to kill me."

Bob sighed. "I'll tell you what I'll do, David, just for you, for nobody else would I do such a deal as this. I'll hit you with eight quarters per package, and that's just because I'm feeling good and because you're a real standup dude. I'll even throw in an ink blotter. How's that? You can dump the six for five bucks apiece, you know you can, and then you either got two to shoot yourself, or you can pick up another ten bucks apiece on the gram. How's that? Have you ever in your life seen such a sport as me?"

"Yeah, I seen such a sport as you. He stands down in the welfare line and picks out old ladies what's picking up their check, he follows them until he sees they've cashed it, and then he rips off their purse. Sometimes, he just kicks them in the back, and picks up their purse when they fall. Yeah, I've seen such a fucking sport as you. Make it nine, and you got a deal."

Bob looked pained. "Nine? Nine fucking quarters you want for some of that talk-talk powder? Wow, man, nine, you sure that ain't milk in them bags and that you ain't trying to burn me? Nine? I wouldn't give you nine quarters a bag for that crap if my old lady had just ODed and that was the only thing that would save her."

The talk of old ladies brought Diane out of the bedroom. She just couldn't contain herself any longer. She had to be in on the action, and if there was going to be any hassling done she wanted to be sure to get her share. Right now she was irked with Bob for even wanting to use the speed, so she instinctively sided with his adversary. "For chrissakes, Bob, give him his nine quarters and get him out of here! I'm getting tired of all this bullshit!"

Bob didn't really mind the intrusion. He was tired of it himself, and it was as good a way as any to cinch the deal. "Okay, pard, nine it is. The little lady's tired, got a headache and wants some peace. So this one time, and this time only, I'll let you take undue advantage of me and give you nine of my lovely little quarters for each bag of crap you got. I'll take all ten."

David's head swiveled back from smiling at Diane so quick you'd have thought he'd just been stung on the side of the face by a wasp. "Ten? What you talking about, man? I'm talking about five. Where do you get that ten shit?"

"I thought you was selling that crap," Bob grinned at him. "You said you had ten bags, didn't you? Fuck it. You don't want to sell them to me, that's okay, then get the fuck out of here."

And with that, Bob started raising the .45 in his hand.

David began backing away. "Look, man, I don't want no shit. I just thought we was talking about five is all, and all of a sudden you're talking about ten, it just threw me, that's all. You want ten, so, okay, you get ten. That's nine apiece, nine times ten, let's see, that's—"

"Seventy-nine," Bob chimed in.

Nadine spoke up for the first time in half an hour. "That's ninety, Bob."

If looks could kill, Nadine would have been dead in a matter of seconds. Everyone in the room, except David, gave her such deadly looks, mixed with utter disgust, that she squirmed and even shuddered. Damn, she thought, she was just trying to be helpful. She knew that most of these people didn't have much in the way of education. All she was doing was trying to help. Still, she knew instinctively without anyone telling her, just as soon as she had opened her mouth, that she had said just about the worst possible thing at the worst possible moment.

David, at least, seemed to appreciate her. He gave her a friendly nod. "Yeah, that's right. Ninety."

Diane gave them all a look of pure disgust and headed for the bedroom to get the pills. While she was gone, David sneaked another glance at Nadine and evidently liked what he saw. "How much you want for her, Bob?" he asked, pointing in her direction.

Bob was thinking of something else, no doubt the pharmacy down on Forty-fifth Street. He looked up, vaguely aware that he had been spoken to. "Huh?"

"How much you want for her, man, the female, the fox, this big lovely stallion you got standing here in your living room?"

Bob turned the pistol on Nadine while he addressed David. "You know what, sport? I'd kill that girl right here and now before I'd sell her to you or any of your kind. What'd you think, I'm some kind of closet pimp, selling dollies I've captured off the fucking farm? Jesus, what kind of animal are you? 'What will you take for her?' I never heard of such a violation of the rights of womanhood in all my goddamn life. You mean you would actually buy the girl here, no questions asked, and take her away?"

David didn't exactly know how to react to some of Bob's quirks, so he merely nodded his head in the affirmative.

"How many bags of speed would you give for her?"

David slumped with relief and headed toward Nadine with his hand extended, ready to feel for himself if all the curves were real and not some fantasy product of female wares some scheming dirty old man had invented and sold to women who felt the need. Rick moved forward to intervene, but Bob motioned him off with his eyes.

David made it all the way to Nadine's side before she spoke. She didn't know whether it was a game or not, but whatever it was, she didn't want any part of it. She stood her ground, chin up and eyes as hard and direct as she could make them. "You little twirp," she said, the little-girl tones gone from her voice. "You come one step closer to me and I'll knock your block off."

David hesitated, looked offended, dropped his hand to his side, and turned back to catch Bob's reaction. Bob said, "What'll you give me for her, twirp? You got ten more bags of that talk-talk powder?"

David was becoming wary. Bob didn't give anything away, and right now he was just too damn eager to deal this broad off. Something was wrong, he figured, he could sense it.

Diane saved the day with her reappearance. She casually threw a cigarette package containing small white pills on the coffee table alongside the ten packages of speed. Bob motioned with his gun toward the table and told David, "Pick up your stuff and go. We got some things to do."

David grabbed the package and started to leave. At the door he turned and reminded Bob, "I like her. I might come back sometime and see you about trading for her."

"Yeah, you do that sometime." Bob nodded, watching his every move.

As soon as David had left, Rick bolted the door and Bob threw his gun on the couch on his way to sit and examine the newly acquired goods. Nadine, still indignant over the insult, announced to no one in particular and everyone in general, "I ain't being sold like no pig in the poke to nobody."

Bob looked up from the speed he was inspecting. "The next time you come to my aid and help me with my math, I'll drag you out by the goddamn hair and sell you to the first one-eyed Filipino I can find, for whatever he'll goddamn give me, even if it's only a goddamn bag of Bull Durham. Now, get the damn spoons and outfits out here and let's shoot some of this speed and just see if we didn't get ourselves burned."

Bob shot a gram, shuddered, coughed, blinked a couple of times, and then said, "Well, I don't guess we got ourselves completely burned, but it could be a little better."

Diane went through a similar ritual with three quarters of a gram. She thought it wasn't shit, but then Diane always thought that.

Rick went with half a gram, snorted, whistled, and added, "Not bad, not bad at all."

They all looked toward Nadine. She stood alone, a stranger caught up in the misery of one who feels rejected from all sides. Finally Rick tried to cheer her up. "Did you ever get that half a blue put away, hon?"

Nadine almost sobbed a "no" and stuck out her hand, revealing the soft, sticky blue mess in her palm.

Bob laughed. "What you trying to do, babe, palm that old pill right off into your bloodstream?"

Diane joined her man in laughter. But Rick looked

even more sympathetic and put his arm around her. "Don't you worry yourself, hon," he said. "We'll get you some more. It wasn't your fault that guy came and disrupted your thing."

Nadine relaxed into the comfort of his arm and leaned her head on his shoulders. "I don't even know if I want any more of that crap, Rick," she said. "I'm tired of vomiting all the time."

That drew a remark from Bob, said in his usual commanding manner. "Don't give her no heavy, Rick, we're going back to work in a few minutes, just as soon as we've cleaned up and relaxed a bit. Just give her a little speed mixed with maybe a piece of a sixteenth. I don't want her sick or worrying about getting that way. We've got work to do this night."

Nadine turned away and went into her bedroom. She just felt she couldn't bear to be ordered around any more that day.

Rick picked up an outfit, a spoon, and the glass of water and followed her. He closed the door and turned to face an incensed Nadine.

"Why's that sonofabitch always got to be ordering us around? He thinks he's king shit. Well, I'll tell you one goddamn thing, Rick, he ain't ordering me around no more, and he ain't standing around talking about selling me to this guy or that guy neither. I'm leaving this dump and I don't care whether you come along or not. And I don't want any more of that crap. Stick them goddamn needles in your own ass!"

Rick placed the paraphernalia by a bedside lamp and turned to her. "Listen, Nadine. That's one of the best people you'll ever run across in your entire life, even if you live to be a hundred. He wasn't going to sell you to that ding, he was just trying to teach you a lesson. If that ding had laid a hand on you, he would have regretted it, I can tell you that. Bob was just aching for that guy to try, I could see it on his face. Man, do you know what that guy would do for you, me, Diane, or anyone in his crew? He'd literally die for you, Nadine, that's what he'd do. Maybe you don't believe me, but I know it's true, just as I know I'm standing right here talking to you this minute. Why do you think he always dives, or is always the first one in with the gun. You know why? Because he just won't ask anyone to do something he won't do himself, that's why. The only reason he always tries to act so mean is because he's so soft he's afraid you and everyone else will find out and take advantage of him. Man, I been hearing about Bob for years. He's a standup dude, one of the best in the trade. He won't let you down. He's famous for that one particular thing, along with a lot of more obvious talents. Don't let him or Diane get you down. They mean well, really they do."

Rick put his arms around Nadine's waist and they locked in a standing, swaying embrace. Nadine seemed to hold back at first, but suddenly she relented, squeezing Rick with all her might and whispering, "I just hope you're right, lover. I just hope you're right."

In a matter of minutes they were back in the car, erratically heading for the downtown area, with Diane behind the wheel. Bob was again alone in the back, going over a mental checklist of things they needed and visualizing their plan of operation.

Up front, Nadine was turned in the seat with her face buried in Rick's shoulder. Among the things she had had enough of for one day was Diane's driving. Rick simply kept his eyes closed and hoped for the best. The best was that they would get there and back without all being killed.

When Diane drove, she spent at least half the time with her head turned to the rear so she could watch Bob. Some people claimed she literally drove by watching what the cars behind her were doing. Bob never criticized her driving unless they were driving home from a score and had drugs in the car, because that was the only time he wanted to avoid involvement in an accident. Otherwise, he was willing to take things as they came. In fact, he loved to get out and holler and scream at other drivers, particularly if they were the ones wronged in the wreck. And because of Diane's driving, this happened quite often. Diane was happy this way because she got to watch Bob and wonder what he was thinking and Bob was happy because sooner or later Diane would do some stupid thing that would give him an opportunity to yell himself hoarse at some unsuspecting driver, who usually didn't quite know what had happened. So everyone was happy except Rick, Nadine, or any other poor fool with no choice but to go with the system, because as long as Bob and Diane were a team, that was the way it was going to be and it was no use to hope otherwise.

In the back, Bob was flat on his back. He couldn't stand to watch Diane's erratic driving or the traffic situations it would sooner or later create either. Bob never admitted to that, though. He simply claimed it was best for all concerned if he lay low, because he was so well known by all the cops and narcos in the city. So even if they happened to spot Diane, they wouldn't see him, and then

they wouldn't be placing him at the scene of any nefari-
ous crime being committed. It was a pretty good theory,
and some fell for it until they rode across town with
Diane driving, and then they knew it was bullshit and
Bob only hid himself away in the back seat because he
was too scared to look.

As they neared the Forty-fifth Street commercial area,
Diane found a place to park by backing into the car
behind them and pushing it ten feet down the street and
then pulling ahead to push the car in front ten feet in the
other direction. Then she backed up again until she was
right up against the car behind. This left a quick exit into
the street should they need it, which they often did. Bob
had taught her this trick years ago when she first learned
to drive.

Before leaving the car, Bob asked, "Okay, everyone
got everything straight about what you're supposed to
do?"

Diane's matter-of-fact "Yeah, we got it straight"
blended in with Rick's more intense "Yeah."

"Rick, you got your mace and smoke grenade?"

"Yeah."

"You got your screaming voice all set to go, Nadine?"

Nadine nodded, but didn't speak. She was so frightened and nervous that she didn't trust her voice to answer without cracking.

"That's what I like about you, Nadine, that scream of
yours. When you cut loose, the hair damn near stands
straight up on my head, and I just know they can hear it
all the way down to city hall."

And then Bob grinned his practiced evil grin. "Well,
hell, let's get on in that store. They ain't going to come

out here to the car and hand us the stuff, you know. We just gotta get off our fat asses and get in there and take it. This one is on me, pards, this one's mine, I can feel it right this minute. That goddamn store is mine, you all hear that? It's mine, and we're just going in there and picking up my narcotics. It ain't stealing, it ain't nothing. It's mine out front and I'm going to get it. Are you with me?"

Back at him came the yeahs and the nods. Diane watched her man; as always, her face glowed with pleasure just watching him and listening to his insane crap. Rick knew what Bob was doing, he was priming them, trying to build up their confidence along with his own. He was pulling them together into a group that would react as one. Nadine thought it was all damn foolishness and wondered if Bob hadn't gone over the edge. Maybe he had some insanity in his family or something, she imagined, with all that talk about how it was his and it wasn't stealing and all of that nonsense.

Bob's drugstore was part of a large convenience store, selling everything from vitamins to sporting goods, with hardware and clothing thrown in. There were at least thirty clerks and eight checkout stands. But the worst part of the whole operation from Bob's point of view was that this store joined a large supermarket that kept a uniformed, armed guard on hand at all times. The pharmacy section was toward the rear of the store on the left-hand side. Three pharmacists and two checkout girls usually worked that section. However, on Saturday nights, only one pharmacist and one checkout girl stayed on the job. That was why Bob had saved this particular store for a hot Saturday night.

The group entered the store and split up. Bob took off purposefully toward the vitamins, which were displayed in front of the Dutch-door entrance to the enclosed area of the pharmacy. He fairly glowed as he moved along. His heartbeat was humming along at 150 per minute, his confidence was unshakable, and everywhere he looked prospects seemed favorable. The pharmacist was draped over the counter talking to an old woman with a shopping bag. The store had enough shoppers in it to keep the clerks busy, but not enough to clutter up his act. Everything was going to be just fine. After all, it was his store, wasn't it? Hell, he could do whatever he wanted in it.

Diane made her way to the opposite corner of the store from Bob, taking up her post by the hardware, curtains, and sporting goods. She glanced frequently toward Bob while fumbling through her purse for the can of lighter fluid. She found it, slipped off the small red cap, and proceeded to soak everything in sight. Alcohol was best because it was hard to detect bright flames, but this evening there hadn't been time to transfer some alcohol to the lighter fluid can. So she was going with plain old lighter fluid. It would work just as well, even if it was a little flashier when ignited.

Rick took up a position near the back of the store, a little more toward Bob's side than Diane's. He looked around to see if anyone was observing him, and when he decided no one was, he took a military smoke grenade out of his pocket, jammed it between items on a shelf, and backed away, letting the string that was attached to the pin run through his hands.

Nadine had the easiest job and she knew it. She placed

herself in a direct line between Diane and Rick and just waited.

When Bob saw that everyone was ready, he gave the signal by reaching up and stroking his chin. Then three things happened simultaneously. Diane lit a match and casually flipped it onto some soaked curtains. Rick jerked the string, which pulled the pin, which released hundreds of cubic feet of smoke in a matter of seconds. And Nadine began to scream. She screamed "Fire, Fire." She screamed like she had never screamed before, and she screamed repeatedly as though she was seized by a frenzy of panic, which of course she was.

Bob nearly gagged laughing in the telling of it later. "It caught on like the bubonic plague. You never seen or heard the likes of it. There was that damn silly Nadine, screaming like she owned the goddamn place, drowning out all other voices combined, except that the movement of the people in the store sounded like a damn herd of elephants all getting up and stampeding off, or maybe like a swarm of bees magnified a thousand times. Everyone was moving, except some were headed the wrong way. People ran right through shelves and over displays, nothing was sacred. And the clerks, they took off with everybody else. If the guy that owned the joint would have been there, he'd have had a hell of a time keeping his head. It damn near caught me up, and shit, I was the one that set the whole thing in motion. I never in my life seen anything like that. People deserted their children and bolted for the doors, pushed their way outside, panicked, rushed back in to try to find the little nippers, and then panicked and ran back out again. That guard in the supermarket ran right along with the rest. By that time

the smoke was getting so thick I was getting a little panicked myself, scared that I might not be able to locate the
narcotics even though I knew where they were kept. Yes-
siree-bob, that there store was certainly mine that night.
I stepped into that pharmacy, made my way back to the
two wooden cabinets that hung on the rear wall, and
there it was, a goddamn fortune to be had for the taking.
There were blues, Dilaudid, morphine, cocaine, Al-
vodine, Pantopon, Desoxyn, Ritalin, Dexedrine,
Preludin, and Percodan. I took the whole damn store,
put it all in the large pocket Diane made for me that
stretches all the way around the inside of my jacket. I
might as well have stopped off and took the money out of
the tills as well, but we still had a little cash stuffed away
and I figured I'd better leave well enough alone. I looked
and sounded like the clinking fat man in the circus.
There I was with all them bulges sticking out. It's a damn
good thing it was so smoky in there or I'd have never
gotten away with it. When I had everything I wanted I
stumbled toward the front door and some Zeke comes
running into the store to help me out. When I finally got
to the car, everyone was there and Diane was as nervous
as a pup trying to crap on the back floor of a moving
automobile. Lord, we sure did get fat that day."

Diane pulled into traffic as soon as Bob closed the car
door. Bob grinned his practiced evil smile back there in
his favorite position, looking like the devil himself with
his smoke-streaked face. And then he began slowly taking various bottles out of his inside pocket and casually
inspecting them. He did this to tease Diane and he did a
thorough job of it. Every time she'd turn around he'd
scream out, "Goddamnit, Diane, get your eyes back on

the road. You wreck this car on the way home and I'll beat your head till it's flat."

Bob screwed up his face in the nastiest expression he could imagine when addressing Diane, but when she turned back to face the road, his anger would fade and the smoke-streaked grin would grow broader still.

Nadine watched all this in fascination. It was then that she decided there was a lot more to Diane and Bob than she had previously suspected. They were very much in love with each other, she thought—yes, very much indeed.

As soon as they were safely home with all the locks secured, they began going through the same ritual as before, with Bob dragging out one bottle at a time. Then they all sat down and shot whatever they felt they could handle.

Once that was over, out came the speed and again they all had to try some of that to see if they might yet squeeze just a few more twinges of pleasure out of their worn-out, drug-soaked bodies.

After that, everyone was nervous, because when you're hooked hard on heavy narcotics, speed doesn't quite hit you the way it does when you're clean. When you're hooked, it hits you harder, makes you nervous, talkative, and keeps you constantly in motion. So now Bob started getting anxious about their haul and all the outfits lying around and he had Diane climb out the bedroom window and bury the whole business, all of it, and when she came back in, he paced the living room floor in one direction and she went back and forth in the other. And both of them carried on a continual stream of conversation with each other and Rick and Nadine as well.

Bob talked of nothing but drugs, all the pharmacies he had taken, how fat they had been and how easy or how much trouble each of the scores had been. Diane countered with talk of her sex life, how it was sagging, how much trouble she was having with her female organs and how much of a dog Bob was for not letting her play a more active role in their wrassling matches with drugstores. She wanted to dive, get the narcotics out of the drawers and off the shelves while the pharmacist was diverted or held by someone else, or hell, even go in with a gun. She wasn't above that; she had done it lots of times while Bob was in prison, she reminded him, and she could do it again if he'd turn her loose. So why couldn't she do it now?

Rick and Nadine sat in utter amazement and watched, nodding from time to time to show they were trying to keep up with both conversations at once, and ohhed when they were supposed to oh, and awwed when they were supposed to aw.

Finally Nadine got tired of the show and began feeling vaguely uncomfortable. Suddenly she realized she was hungry and hadn't had a bite to eat the whole day. She looked up and asked everyone in general, "When we going to eat? Don't you people ever eat?"

The others looked at her as if she were crazy.

"Eat, eat," Diane repeated. "What do you want to eat for?"

Bob smiled and motioned toward the kitchen. "There's some peanut butter and bread in the reefer, probably some milk, too, and if that don't suit you, get your old man to run down to a hamburger joint and get you something. Have him get me a chocolate shake while he's at it."

Nadine looked disgusted. "Don't you people ever sit down and eat a regular meal?"

Diane sighed. "Yeah, I stop by the chicken joint sometimes and buy a bucket of chicken and some ice cream."

"Chicken, ice cream, hamburgers, is that all you people ever eat?"

"Yeah, I kind of like ice cream," Bob grinned. "Don't you like ice cream?"

Nadine turned to Rick. "Will you go out and get me something to eat?"

"Okay, okay, honey. What do you want? You'd better make out a list so I don't forget nothing when I get there."

So Rick left with a list. Thirty minutes later he returned with a grocery bag cradled in his arm.

"Anybody hungry?"

Nadine ran up to him and peeked in the bag. Then they pranced into the kitchen like a couple of giggly teenagers. Bob and Diane looked at each other in amazement, then broke out laughing.

Bob's laugh died prematurely, however. His face straightened up suddenly, he got a funny look in his eye, and he abruptly turned and blew into the kitchen like a warm summer breeze.

"Here, let me have that food, I'll fix you up a meal."

And he elbowed his way between Nadine and the electric stove.

Confused, Nadine protested. "No, I can do it." But then she noticed that gleam in his eye, and instead of feeling put upon, as she might have before, she giggled,

appreciating him now and figuring that she was probably
going to get her dinner and a clown act as well.

"Did Diane ever tell you," Bob said to Rick, as he
stooped and lunged, pulling out pots and pans and
knives, "that I was a cook in the army? That's right," he
emphasized, as Rick started cracking up, "four years
slaving over the hot stove, damn near picked myself up a
medal of honor and a Purple Heart serving up those
flapjacks and sizzling those sausages."

By now he was running water over potatoes and starting to slice them into a pan.

"Here, you better use some oil," Nadine laughed,
handing him the vegetable oil.

"Oh, yeah, oil."

Diane stood in the entrance to the kitchen, her hands
on her hips, elbows out. "You never were in the goddamn army, you fucking liar."

Bob ignored her and kept working, but moments later
he stopped, stiffened, and asked the women, "Isn't there
an apron here somewhere?" And he began diving at the
cupboards and drawers. "Don't you ladies keep an apron
around?" he added, as all he found in those drawers and
cupboards, besides an occasional pan, plate, glass, or
fork, was air space. "Shit, what kind of a kitchen is this?"

And Rick and Nadine laughed all the harder as Bob
said, "Well, I guess I'll just have to improvise. The ladies,
they don't keep no apron," and he unbuttoned his shirt,
slipped it off, and tied it hastily around his waist.

Diane started to get into the mood too. She allowed
herself a quiet smile and just stood there, awed, watching
her man, getting more and more worked up, having the
hardest time containing her wonder and admiration.

And Bob worked on, whipping up a halfway respectable meal, and setting it out on the table. But he didn't get a chance to eat it himself, except for what he managed to nibble in the cooking process. For as soon as he set the plates and food on the table, she leaped on him from behind, and despite his protests—"What the fuck are you doing? The goddamned bitch has gone completely crazy"—dragged him off to their bedroom and pushed and wrestled him onto the bed.

Bob forgot about the food, but he wasn't ready to give in yet. "What do you want to go to bed for? Man, we ought to be out working. I know this little old hospital up in this small town on the coast, and it's a virgin, I know it is, ain't never had the cold hand of grand theft put on it yet. What a bird's nest on the ground. I mean, this place has got security zero. They ain't got but two cops in the whole town. One works the breakfast-to-supper shift and the other catches the supper-to-midnight gig. From then on it's free. They ain't got but one nurse that works there most nights, unless they have a big wreck out on the highway or some such shit and have to call in a bunch of doctors. And the pharmacy, you should see it. It sits right down in the basement in between the central supply and this little old laundry they got. Jesus, all we got to do is saw the bars off the window, open her up, and slip right on in. I'll bet they got coke, mammy, all those hospitals hold big-time coke."

"You're crazy, Bob, do you know that? You ain't fucked me in a month and you're crazier than a shithouse rat. You ain't got a lick of sense. We just pulled off two of the best scores we've made in months and off you trot looking to find more. Don't you know when to take a break?

Why don't you let me dive next time? I'm as good as you and you know it. I've even heard you tell people I'm better than you are. Why don't you let me dive, Bob? Goddamnit, I'm sick of standing around coughing and driving the car and not getting fucked. You know me, honey, I can't stand to go on forever like this. Why don't you roll over and lay down on the bed for a while and just hold me?"

"Hold you? What do you want me to hold you for? Man, we ought to get cracking, get in the car and see if we can't make it up to that hospital before it gets daylight out. Boy, you'll just love this one, Diane. I'll even let you hacksaw some on the bars."

"Oh boy, you'll let me hacksaw the bars. Whoopee. For chrissakes, you mean you're not even going to let me go inside? Jesus Christ, and I thought you loved me. You won't fuck me and you won't let me go inside. What kind of an animal are you? You just think of yourself, that's all you ever do. You don't care nothing about me or anybody else. All you care about is those damn pharmacies and yourself. How do you think I feel, knowing I haven't contributed my share and that it's always your big deal and I'm left out in the cold or chauffeuring you all around. Well, fuck you, Bob Hughes. I'm going off on my own. I know lots of people that would take me on their crews. I never had a bit of trouble when you were in prison. I shot all the dope I wanted and I did whatever I wanted to do."

"Aw, forget all that crap, Diane. Let's go on up the coast right now and just look over this hospital, if nothing else. I mean, you'll just cream your jeans when you see it. It sits way back in the woods. It ain't no trouble making an approach or finding a place to park. It's a giveaway, baby, I can feel how it feels to be standing in that pharmacy right now. I can actually see all those big gallon jugs of pills on the shelves. Thousands of them, baby, thousands of them. Just think of it, just close your eyes and look at it. Coke by the twenty-ounce jug! Can you imagine twenty ounces of coke? Did I ever tell you about the time we got the hospital over east of the mountains and got the twenty-ounce jug of coke?"

Diane looked at him in disgust. "Only about ten thousand times," she said.

Meanwhile, after eating, Rick and Nadine had gone to their own bedroom and began their evening simply by smiling at each other. Rick felt good because he sensed Nadine was happy, and Nadine was beginning to feel like maybe she belonged in the group, like she was wanted and her feelings were being considered, even if it only amounted to a good square meal now and then.

Finally Rick said, "Lord, they sure can carry on."

Nadine nodded, then looked slightly puzzled and asked, "Is he really crazy enough to try and drag us all up the coast this morning?"

"Hell, I don't know." Rick shook his head. "You never can tell what he might do. And I suppose if he really wants to, that we will go. You can never really tell when he's serious, though. A lot of the crap he says and pulls, he does just to tease Diane, so you never really know what he's got in the back of his mind. Sometimes I'd swear there was nothing at all there, and then I see him in action and the way he organizes every detail and then I know he's got to have something going for him somewhere. Sometimes he'll pull stunts that you just know have got to be the most insane moves you ever heard of, but then when you see how well it all works out, and get to thinking about it, you begin to see a pattern in it all. The guy's not a fool. At least, as far as getting what he wants, he's not. He'll no doubt kill himself in the next couple of years if the cops don't get him first. But I'll bet you one goddamn thing. I'll bet you a dollar he dies happy, either pulling off a good narcotics coup or going out the back door the easy way with an overdose."

"What do you mean, the easy way? Dying's dying, there ain't no easy way! Once you're dead, you're dead, ain't you?"

"I don't think so, baby. If I thought so, I wouldn't be doing what-all I'm doing now. Oh, I don't know, narcotics aren't everything, not to me, not yet. I could live without it if I had to. But why should I do that? To tell the truth, I like the excitement, I love to watch Bob work, I like the lifestyle. I love everything about this whole scene. I even love to hear Diane talk about her sex life, even though it does get embarrassing at times."

Rick took Nadine's hand and looked at her lovingly. Nadine blushed despite herself, looked down, and reached for him. Her head jerked upright and her body froze at the sound of the front door being ripped away from its hinges and crashing to the apartment floor.

"What the fuck was that?" Rick reacted, bolting upright.

Four burly narcotics detectives came galloping across the downed door like a bunch of mustangs breaking out of a corral.

Guns drawn, faces tight, muscles coiled, they paired

off into two teams and simultaneously kicked in the
doors to both bedrooms.

Bob had been lying on the bed next to Diane. She had
finally coaxed him into snuggling up beside her and
holding her. The crash brought them to their feet beside
the bed. Bob's first instinct was to go for his gun, but
when he realized he had no gun with him in the bedroom, he just gave up and decided, what the hell, let fate
play as it may. So when Detectives Halamer and Gentry
burst into the bedroom, Bob was standing there, trying
to look as much at ease as possible, wearing nothing but
a smile, with Diane, also bare-assed and topless, scared
and clinging to his right arm.

It was obvious they were neither armed nor carrying
any narcotics on their persons. But narco bulls being
what they are, they have their little ritual to go through,
whether their subjects are naked or passed out dead to
the world or sick and vomiting. They've got their thing to
do and they do it.

Gentry did the talking, ordering Bob and Diane up
against the wall for a shakedown. Once that was out of
the way, he ordered both Bob and Diane to turn around
and began making snide remarks about their appearance.

"Getting a little droopy there in the tits, ain't you,
Diane?"

By now Diane had relaxed into it, seeing that Bob
didn't look too worried. She looked down at her breasts,
and after scanning them awhile, smiled and said, "Yeah,
it's that goddamn Bob's fault. He won't take them out for
exercise anymore."

Gentry smiled and turned to Bob. "What's the matter,

Bob? You been shooting too much dope again? Seems like the last time we was by here and you was hooked to the gills, Diane was complaining of the same thing."

"Oh, you know how it is," Bob came back. "Out on the job all day, work, work, work like a dog, man comes home, he wants to relax a bit, don't want to be jumping up and down like a kid waiting to go to the bathroom. You guys ought to know how it is."

"About all that work, Bob. We been hearing about all that work you've been doing. I was just saying to my partner the other day, looks like old Bob Hughes has finally slowed down a bit, we hadn't had a bad report on you in days. And then wham bam, you knock off two, one in the morning and one in the afternoon, burn up half a store, panic the people, and raise all kinds of hell. Didn't you sort of expect us to drop by?"

"Hey, wait a minute, that wasn't me, pal. I ain't hit no poison shop in years. Look at me. Do I look like I'm using?"

"Looks like you're hooked to the gills, and we got witnesses this time, Bob. Oh boy, do we ever have witnesses. We got the guy that helped you out of that burning store this morning. He recognized you right off. Looked at your picture and said, definitely, that's the man."

"You got a warrant, pal?"

"Yeah, I got a warrant, Bob. We put them on micro dots now. You know what a micro dot is, it's a little photograph, about the size of a Dilaudid pill. I got it pasted right on the end of the thirty-eight slug that's lined up in the barrel of this gun right now. You want to see it, Bob? I'll stick this gun right up to your ear and shoot it through. If you'll just turn your eyes backward, and if you're fast enough, you can read it when it passes through, Bob."

"Wow, man, you guys are heavy. What you been reading, Mickey Spillane? I thought they kept you guys busy, out catching them big-time wheeler dealers that run around here selling those little packages of milk sugar. What do you do with that crap when you buy it, anyway, take it back to the station to use in the office coffee?"

Gentry motioned toward the door with both his head and gun. "How about that pretty little girl in the other bedroom, Bob? Is she hooked good? Is she going to slobber, puke, shake, and sneeze if we take her in and hold her, huh, Bob? Is she going to sing real good for us? I hear she's a hell of a screamer, Bob. In fact, I thought I heard something myself, clear down at the station. I didn't know of course that you'd went completely mad and were trying to burn up half the town. You know what they give little punks like you for arson? They give them life, Bob. That's first-degree arson when you set a fire and there's people in the building. You've just parlayed a chickenshit heeling beef into the number-one monster of them all, and we got us a witness that puts you right on the spot. What do you say to that, Bob?"

"What can I say? Let me call my attorney. I'm sure he can straighten all this out in a few minutes."

"No, Bob, no attorney this time. No warrant, no attorney, we're just looking around for the stuff. We can get the warrant tomorrow. What the hell, there ain't no hurry. You ain't going nowhere, not as hooked as you are. Where could you go? Now, where you got the crap hid? You ain't went out in the bushes and buried it again, have you, Diane?"

Diane was beginning to get fed up with standing there naked. "Fucker, I don't know what you're talking about. Why don't you just go piss up a rope."

"Diane, what language you use." Gentry looked to his partner, pretending to be shocked, and then turned to Bob. "What's the matter, Bob, can't you do anything with her anymore? I always heard that you guys had class."

"Oh, hell, you know how it is," Bob shrugged. "What with all that women's-lib crap going on every day and the news media full of it, what can you expect? They say that a woman's got a right to say what she wants nowadays, and who am I to say any different?"

"Okay, kiddies, here's how it's coming down. You can just tell us where it's at and save yourselves a whole lot of trouble or you can sit there with your mouths shut while we tear this apartment apart board by board. Now, how's it going to be?"

Bob smiled his "what can I say—it's out of my hands" smile and said, "Tear away. This place is rented and insured and my agent will no doubt file against you, because, pard, you ain't finding nothing in this apartment unless you brought it with you and plan to plant it on us, and even if you do, I'll beat it in court on illegal search and seizure and then I'll sue the crap out of you and your whole department. So just shoot your best lick."

And that's what they proceeded to do. They brought in fire axes and attacked the walls. They smashed the furniture, doing a particularly thorough job on the large color television set in one corner of the living room. And what they couldn't smash, they tore. There wasn't one item of clothing that was spared, not even one dish rag left intact. When the detectives left hours later, with their axes and pruning shears over their shoulders, Diane, Bob, Rick, and Nadine sat huddled in a corner of the living room, stark naked on a pile of rags.

Bob and Diane were beginning to get withdrawal symptoms. Normally, withdrawal wouldn't have caught up with them so soon, but in this case the speed had been working its best to rid their bodies of its opposite number. So Bob and Diane sat and yawned, sneezed, and occasionally watched one of their arms or legs jerk outward in a frantic, convulsive movement.

Rick felt depression, the depression of a lack of drugs combined with the added discomfort of sitting on a debris-covered floor. He looked around at the completely destroyed apartment. "You going to sue them, Bob? I'd sue the hell out of them if it was up to me."

Bob lifted his head off his arms slowly. He yawned and wondered how long it would be before the yawns would leave his mouth cramped open. Finally he said, "Sue them? Hell no, I ain't going to sue them. I told you all this crap was rented and insured. What do I want to sue them for?"

"How about our clothes?"

"Clothes, them rags? Fuck them rags, we can always go out and shoplift some more. Hell, I stole these and I can steal others. They ain't costing me nothing, they are just taxing the stores. Hell, they can tear my clothes up all day long if they want to, every goddamn day of the week and I still wouldn't sue them, and they know it. Hell,

man, that would be just like sticking your finger in a
hornet's nest just because you didn't like hornets. Shit, I
love them cops, them's the only thing we got between us
and complete destitution. What do you think would happen if there weren't no mean, hot-shot cops? Why, we'd
have so much competition there wouldn't be nothing left
to steal. It's getting to be almost that bad anyway, what
with all those ringy square-johns out there sticking a
pistol in everybody's face. Hell, yeah, I pray every night
that the cops will get smarter and get more money for
more equipment to catch more of those square-johns
with. Man, love your police force. I used to have a
bumper sticker that said just that. Whatever did we do
with that car, Diane?"

"That's the one the guy in the big truck hit me in, you
remember? That was the time you jumped out and hollered, 'Watch where you're driving, you big drunk freak,'
and he got out of his truck, and he was big, and you just
had to go and scream at him some more, and so he hit
you a couple of times. You remember that, Bob? That
was when we had to take you to the hospital, you had
those busted ribs and that big lump on your head and the
broken arm. Surely you remember the broken arm, Bob?
They put a cast on you that ran clean to the end of your
fingertips, and you couldn't use that arm to fix with, and
you had to depend on me to help you. Remember all the
things I blackmailed you into doing before I'd fix you?
Surely you must remember that broken arm, Bob?"

Bob smiled his practiced evil smile at Diane and said,
"Yes, I do believe I remember that broken arm now that
you mention it. I sure did love that old car, though.
Remember when we took it south and made all those

pharmacies on the coast? Boy, what a car. It was built like a regular army tank. It was one of those big old gas-burning Buicks. Diane crashed into, and ran over, under, and through the middle of everything along the road between here and California. And talk about fat pharmacies, you remember that one you just drove through the side of? And while we was there, I looked out the window of the car, and there was the narcotics drawer, pretty as you please, with a little white card on its front saying so. I just reached out the car window, slid the drawer out, and then you just backed out and off we roared into the sunset."

"Yeah, but that pharmacy was a flimsy-built little old thing, though. You'd never get away with that anymore."

Bob and Diane seemed to run out of things to say. Only gloom and an occasional fit of sneezing crept into the silence. Finally Diane looked up at Bob, the concern evident on her face, and asked, "What are we going to do now?"

Bob thought for a few seconds, then answered, "Diane, you go on upstairs and use Old Lady Hart's phone, call your stupid sister, and have her bring us enough clothes to go around."

The opportunity to bite back at Bob seemed to bring Diane to life. "And why do I have to go phone bare-assed naked like I am? And just why does my sister have to be stupid? She don't have no goddamn cops coming in and tearing up her place just because her old man does a good job down at the plant."

"All right, go call your smart sister, then; and you got to call because the only one that would be up at this hour of the morning is likely to be Old Lady Hart, and I just don't think it would be proper for me to go up there with this speed-shriveled-up prick of mine, what looks like a lost angleworm hiding in a chicken factory and giving that old woman any more reason to pity you. You know how you hate pity, Diane."

"Wow, I didn't think you cared. I'll go make the goddamn call, but only on one condition. You either got to fuck me when I get back, or you got to let me go in that hospital pharmacy with you when we get it."

"I'll let you go in the pharmacy with me, you goddamn ding. Now, get up there and make that call."

When Diane's smart sister entered the gutted apartment an hour later with an armload of clothing, the whole group was huddled in a bedroom fixing some narcotics and speed that Diane had dug up. She let out a loud whistle of amazement as she walked through the rubble and into the bedroom. "Good God," she said, "what did they use, sledgehammers?"

"No, fire axes," Diane replied, looking up momentarily from the solution she was drawing through a small wad of cotton in a bent, blackened spoon.

"Christ, I've seen tornadoes down south that didn't produce results as disastrous as this," the smart sister went on.

"Well, I don't suppose they were as concentrated," Bob said. "If those cops had attacked the whole building instead of just this apartment, I don't imagine we'd have caught so much of the main blast."

"No, I guess you're right," the smart sister agreed. "I just didn't think of it like that. By the way, Bob, whatever happened to your prick? Diane, what have you been doing to your man? Or did those cops jump on it too? Have you still got one, Bob, or is it just in hiding?"

Bob looked disgusted and pained, and glared, not at Diane's smart sister, but at Diane. "That's why I asked you to call your dumb sister first," he said.

"Oh, my, my, and such a temper too. I've always had a theory about men with short tempers, that it might follow a pattern, that everything about them was short as well, and now I know there must be something to it."

Bob came right back. "If you ever had a theory in your life, it was poked into you by one of those dirty-old-men professors out at that college you work for. What do you do out there now anyway, smarty, teach one of those abnormal sexual education courses?"

"Witty, oh boy, Bob, you're really on top of it all tonight, and that's what I always liked about you. Of course, what with you being in prison more than half the time messing around with those homosexuals, the family and I don't get to see much of you. Why don't you just leave Diane, Bob, and go join one of those female impersonator clubs? You shouldn't have any trouble at all getting a membership, from what I can see, and then you'd no doubt be happy, not having to use narcotics since you'll finally have found your place in life, learning to enjoy contributing to a normal segment of our community."

"Get her out of here, Diane, get her out! I've never hit one of your female relations yet and I don't want to start tonight. Besides, how can you hit a bitch that's all hole?" And with that, Bob stuck his tongue out at Diane's sister in little-kid fashion and hurriedly strode to the bathroom to get out of range of the barrage of insults he knew would be forthcoming.

Diane's smart sister smiled and raised her voice. "That's what I always liked about old Bob. He just won't stand around to lose. He'll run every time, the yellow-bellied, short-pricked sonofabitch."

She dropped the clothing on the littered floor and headed for the door, saying, "Good-bye, Diane, and be sure to call your stupid sister next time. I've done my good deed for the month."

Diane looked up from another solution she had cooking in a spoon. "Yeah, thanks, smarty," she said. "Sorry I couldn't be more sociable, but what can one do when one doesn't even have a chair to offer?"

They were presentable enough to appear in public after picking through the clothes. As soon as everyone was done fixing, Bob told Nadine and Rick, "You two take the car and go look for an apartment. Get one over on the west side. We haven't hit nothing over there in weeks, so things ought to be cool over there. Diane and I will go over to my mom's in a taxi and get some clothes I left over there. Okay?"

Nadine and Rick nodded in unison and went on their way, happy to be away from Bob and Diane for a while and grateful that they could walk away from the police intrusion and ruined apartment in one piece and apparently still free.

Diane went upstairs to use Old Lady Hart's phone and soon she and Bob were in a taxi heading for his mother's house. Diane wasn't exactly excited about the prospect of hassling with relatives at this particular time, but Bob assured her his mom didn't mean any harm. Diane, of course, had heard this before, but still she had never come away from encounters with the woman reassured about her chosen way of life and her choice of Bob as her man.

At the front door, Diane winced as the door swung wide open and Bob's mother gasped, throwing her hand to her mouth, and then announced to the world, "Oh Lord, it's my dope-fiend thieving son and his crazy nymphomaniac wife. Hide the silverware, hide the medicine in all the cabinets, hide the TV, and don't let your purse out of your hand."

"Jesus, Mama, when have I ever stole anything out of your house? Name me one thing I ever took from you without telling you? Just name me one thing?"

"I never said you took nothing, you needle freak. I'm just repeating what they say on the TV, and as many times as they say it, it must be true. And look at all the times you've been in prison. I know the state hasn't supported you for half your life because you're so good. You're a menace, Robert, you're a filthy, thieving menace, and all us good people have to pay for your good times with added taxes. They said that on the TV too."

"Oh yeah, well, I'll just have to drag that goddamn TV out of here if you keep on watching that junk. Why don't you watch all those murder mysteries and horror stories like normal people do?"

"Oh, my God," Bob's mother said, throwing up her hands and walking back into the house as Bob and Diane followed. "Please, please God, tell me what I did to deserve bringing into this world a thieving, pleasure-seeking tramp without even a lick of sense? What have I done to deserve the agony, the disgrace; never knowing

when there's going to be a knock on the door and someone telling me my baby's dead, green with an overdose
of some drug, shot by a mad pharmacist, or run down by
a car while fleeing from police pursuit? Why me? What
could I have possibly done to deserve all this?''

Diane had the answer. "You was probably just too
strict, Mrs. Hughes. If you hadn't yelled at him for playing with himself when he was a child, he probably would
have done it more, got much bigger with the exercise,
and turned out to be a perfectly normal person. That's
what my sister thinks, anyway, and she's a professor of
psychology out at the university.''

For once Mrs. Hughes was stopped. She stared at Diane, dumbfounded that she would think such a thing and
even more amazed that she would have the nerve to say
it.

Bob intervened with his request. "Say, Mama, do you
by chance still have those clothes Diane and I left here
when we both got sent to the joint that time?''

Mama stood in thought for a few seconds, then said,
"No, Robert, I gave all that stuff away years ago. Let me
see, who did I give it to? Was it the garbage man? No, it
must have been somebody else. I can't remember who it
was, Robert. So now what are you going to do, go snitch
me off to the police, get me arrested for stealing your
clothes and giving them away? No, of course not, my
boy's not a snitch, did you know that, Diane? He won't
even tell on them people who tell on him. Says it's professional pride that keeps him from it. I remember once
when he was just a baby and got caught red-handed in a
drugstore over on Tenth Street. Everyone else got away
but him. They all took off in a car and left him running

toward the front of the store. So I went down along with
the priest and got it all fixed up, and they said they'd let
him go if he'd just tell who the rest of his pals were, and
do you think he'd do it? No, he wouldn't. He told me
right to my face, 'I can't, Mama, them's my friends.' What
kind of friends could they possibly have been? They left
him. And me, his mama, his own flesh and blood, the
person that babied him, changed his diapers, and held
him while he was sick, would he do that one favor for me?
No, no, no. And so right then I disowned him, Diane. He
is no longer a son of mine. He is a thief and a dope fiend
and that is more important to him than I am, and so we
are finished, finished I tell you, and never again do I go
down and try to make deals for him. He can go to prison.
He likes it there anyway, don't you, Robert?"

"If you say so, Mama." Bob nodded absentmindedly.
"I'm going up to look in the attic. I think you forgot
about the clothes I'm talking about."

Mrs. Hughes threw up her hands again. "And so now
I'm a forgetful liar as well. Oh, the pain my own flesh and
blood has brought home to me, the disgrace. How can I
ever live down the disgrace?" She groaned in despair,
then turned on Diane. "I'd ask you to sit down, Diane,
but the last time I did that you fell asleep and dropped a
burning cigarette on my couch and burned a hole in it.
So if you'd please, just stand where you are so I can
watch you, so I can catch you should you fall asleep
standing on your feet. I wouldn't want you to burn yourself up or fall down and hurt yourself while you are in my
home, Diane."

"Why do you hate Bob and I so, Mama?" Diane asked,

looking pained. "We never done anything to make you hate us so."

"I don't hate you, Diane, and I don't hate Robert either, and the good Lord knows 'that to be the truth. I truly feel pity for both of you. I feel pity for both of you because you have so much to give, and you both don't know how to give, all you know is how to take. You think, but you always think wrong. There are so many more things to do in this world, Diane, than think wrong and take. There are so many things that would bring pleasure to you both, bring you both closer together and closer to God. What do you think God is going to say to you, Diane? When you come up before Him, do you think He's going to welcome you with open arms for doing wrong all of your life? Do you think He is going to love you for abandoning your young children to someone else's care? Do you think you are going to stay young and live forever, Diane? You're not babies anymore. Then, I could excuse you both by saying it was just the ignorance of youth. But no more. You're grown up now, and yet you still act like children who want to do nothing but run and play. You cannot run and play all your life, Diane. Someday it is all going to catch up with you, the abuse you have given your body and mind. It will catch up to you eventually, Diane, and then you will either die and pay for your sins by burning in hell or end up in the crazy house. And there you will stay, a crazy, lonely old woman. I know, Diane. You think I'm dumb just because I am old and square. Don't you think people did your same kind of things when I was young? I've seen it all, Diane. I'm not so dumb as you think."

About this time Bob emerged with two suitcases and

clothes draped across his shoulders. "I found them, Mama," he announced. "They were up in the attic behind all the furniture you got stored there."

"Good, good, I'm glad I didn't find them to give away. If I had found them they would have been gone. Is there anything else that belongs to you up there?"

"I don't think so, Mama," Bob said, lowering his eyes to avoid his mother's baleful glare. "If there is, give it away. I can always get some more."

"Oh, to be sure, you'll just go out and steal some more. Did I ever tell you, Diane, about the time he gave me the washer and dryer for Christmas? Oh, they were so nice. No more wringing out the clothes, no more having to empty tubs of dirty water. But you know what, Diane? Now I've got to drop in a quarter every time I want to do the wash. Oh, he pried the front of the cash drawer off so I get my quarter back, but what would my friends say, should they see such a thing? What would the police say if they came around searching the house for Robert like they used to and saw the coin slots in those machines? I know what they would say, they'd say, 'Mrs. Hughes, it's off to jail you go, because it's against the law to have a washing machine with a place for the quarter and dime.' And every time I see a police car drive down our street, Diane, I have to go run down the stairs to the basement to be sure the clothes are hanging just right over them, so if the police come searching my home they won't see the quarter and dime slots. Why do the police always search my home? I ask you that, Diane. They don't search my friends' homes, my neighbors'. They don't get visits from the police in the middle of the night with a warrant to search their homes. Only me, only me. Why has God sought me out and punished me so? What could I possibly have done to deserve all this?"

Bob shuffled from foot to foot. Finally he announced, "Well, we got to go, Mama. See you again soon. You be good now, and don't do anything I wouldn't do."

"And what could I possibly do that you are not capable of, I ask you that?" his mother went on. "What sins could I possibly do that you have not done a thousand times? Get out of my house and take your crazy wife with you! Take her home and wash her mouth out with soap and water, Robert. You hear me, wash your wife's mouth out with soap and water!"

By now, Bob and Diane were out the door and walking down the front steps. Bob looked depressed, as he always did when he left his mother standing at the door, crying out her frustration to the neighborhood. And Diane was not so much angry as agonized and annoyed, as if an arthritic shoulder were acting up again, and no matter how much the sun shone, the pain would never completely go away.

Three days later, Bob, Diane, Nadine, and Rick were established in a new apartment. They had shoplifted enough clothes to keep them all in the height of style on a round-the-world cruise if they should fancy to take one, and they had purchased a used car. They left the old one abandoned with the keys in it, in hopes that some kids would come along, steal it, and keep it moving around town. That way the police would be led astray if they happened to be following it or looking for it. And where would Bob and his crew be? Not in town at all, but down on the coast checking out that virgin hospital that lay there so quietly back in the woods.

"Do I have to go?" Nadine got up the courage to ask. "You're not going to want a screamer or shimmy girl on this one, are you? They always got those signs around hospitals that says QUIET, and if I was to go into that shimmy act, they'd probably throw me in the psycho ward and I'd never get out."

Bob had just followed a big dose of Dilaudid with some of David's speed. He felt good. His whole body hummed a glowing tune that was so beautiful, so quiet, and so soothing that only he could hear it. At times like this, when Bob felt good, really good, he could be as nice and obliging as you please. He fielded Nadine's question and juggled it around in his mind for a while. No, it didn't look like it'd take more than three hands to knock off that hospital. And besides, Nadine could really be a drag, especially when she didn't feel all that good to begin with.

"Yeah, why the hell not," he finally said. "You just go ahead and stay here, Nadine. Just don't answer the door and don't go out unless you positively have to. We haven't got a phone here, so you won't be bothered by that. Just lay around and relax, watch a little TV and get to feeling better. You just wait until we come back. You're going to see the damnedest collection of narcotics you'll ever hope to see in your life. Besides, there's always another hospital. It won't be like if you miss this one you'll miss them all. I'll no doubt spot or hear of another again pretty soon, and if it's as good as this one, we'll go get it, just like we're going after this one right now. Hot dog! I can just see all those pretty colored bottles of pills that hospital is holding for me right now."

Nadine's eyes lit up. "Oh, speaking of dogs, Bob, do

you think Rick and I could get a dog, a little pup or
something, so I'll have something to hold and pet when
you guys are gone?" Nadine spoke daintily, in her little-
girl manner.

"Nope, no dogs, and that's final," Bob shot back.

"What you got against dogs, Bob?" Rick joined in, not
so much because he wanted one, but because he didn't
quite like the way Bob had cut off his woman's request
without even so much as an explanation.

"No fucking dogs!"

The finality of his voice chilled them all.

"Tell them what happened to the last one we had,
Bob," Diane finally said, trying to break the mood and
bring in a note of understanding.

Suddenly Bob felt bad. Everything was going wrong,
his good glow was gone, the sweet song of the poppies
had drifted away. His head began to throb and ache from
the large dose of speed he had taken. He sat down on the
couch and put his head in his hands. "If you want them to
know, Diane, you tell them," he said.

Diane looked over at Bob, her concern apparent, then
turned back to Rick and Nadine. "Well, we had a dog
once, it was a cockapoo. Cutest little pup you ever did
see. Bob stole him out of a car we passed in the street. He
saw that little dog and just knew that he had to have him.
He stepped right over and broke that car's window right
in front of everybody just to get that little feller. And that
pup would follow Bob wherever he'd go, and if we went
out and left him alone, he'd just lay down by the door
and cry until we came home. Got so we had to start hiring
kids to baby-sit the damn thing.

"One time a cop that was shaking down our pad kicked

him, and I never seen Bob get so mad. He jumped right
on that cop and would have beat him to a pulp if those
other cops hadn't came in and drug him off. That was the
only fight I knew that Bob was going to win. Lord, was he
mad.

"Anyway, one night we was cruising a small town
south of here looking for a drugstore to crash. We was
hell on just crashing them in those days. You know, he'd
just throw a garbage can through the front window, dive
in, get the drawer, and then get out. I'd be sitting parked
in front with the engine running. So we spots this poison
shop and it don't look too bad, you know, not good
either, because none of them are really good in a small
town, not for crashing anyway—hell, the police station is
usually only a block, block and a half away.

"Anyway, we'd maybe cruised this particular one three
or four times and Bob, he had his window rolled down so
he could see, since it was raining and misty as hell. So
finally he says to me, 'This is it, it's mine.' I stops the car
and he jumps out with a crowbar and smashes out the
glass in the front window and off he jumps into the joint.

"Well, I see Panda trying to get out the rolled-down
window, and when I make a lunge for him, my foot came
off the brake and the damn car leaps up on the curb and
we start taking out parking meters. I had to get back
under the wheel and get back in control of the car and by
then that damn silly dog had jumped to the sidewalk and
had run through the hole in the glass window to be at
Bob's side. Bob had got the drawer, looked down to see
the dog, and scooped him up as he ran for the car.

"By then, I had the car under control and backed up to
where I was supposed to be. They got out okay and away

we went, and not a moment too soon neither, 'cause
there came the patrol car right after our ass. Oh God, I
never did think we'd get away. We never would have,
either, but I tried to take a corner too fast, lost control of
the car, and around we slid, ending up going backward
down the highway for at least fifty feet. The cop, he came
racing right for us and had to swerve like hell to keep
from hitting us head on.

"Anyway, away we went again, and Bob thought that
we had better throw the stash. So I found a little dirt road
that headed out into the brush, drove up it a ways, and
cut my lights while Bob took the stuff out into the brush
to hide it. He got back in the car and everything was fine.
Except we now either had to go back through the town
we had just ripped off or head in the direction of that cop
that was chasing us. We elected to go back through the
town, because the cop had seen us and we didn't think
the town had a very good description of us yet.

"So, what happened? They got us right in front of the
drugstore, pulled us over, and shook down the car. By
that time, there was cops all over the place, and one of
them happened to spot Panda's bloody footprints in the
drugstore. He must have cut his foot when he jumped in
the store amidst all that broken glass. So off we go to jail.
We both tried like hell to get Panda out on bail and in one
of our friends' care. But the cops, they wouldn't go for
that. They said no, that he was a material witness and
would have to stay in the pound until we went to trial.

"Bob was arranging to have him busted out. He had
contacted some friends and they were going to do it. And
then we went to a preliminary hearing, and what do you
suppose they brought in to use against us as evidence?

Panda's head and feet, that's what. They said he had died
from an infection in his cut foot. I never did believe the
sonsofbitches. I screamed and screamed until they tied
me in a chair and gagged me, and every time they
brought that poor pup's head and feet into that court-
room, I struggled to scream some more."

Nadine looked green and on the verge of tears. "Why
did they ever bring the poor dog's head in?" she asked.
"I can see why they brought the legs, but why the head?"

Bob looked up in disgust. "They brought the head in,
Nadine, to show what was attached to the legs and so all
the people of that good town could say, 'Yes, that's the
dog they had with them, all right.' And perhaps they
brought it in to watch Diane scream, because it was so
obvious she was screaming us right down that hot slip-
pery slide called justice. I mean, if you scream in despair
every time they bring your dead puppy into court, there's
not going to be much doubt in the jury's mind that the
dog did belong to you. Also, Diane didn't just scream,
she screamed, 'Oh, you motherfuckers, I'll kill you, you
sorry, slimy motherless bastards,' and other such quaint
little gutter spiels, and that is what got us sent to the
penitentiary. Diane got two and a half years and I got
five, and I never said a word. I never could quite figure
that out, but hell, who can figure the law? They'll give a
child molester six months in the county jail and turn
around the same day and send some poor sick dope fiend
to the state penitentiary for eighty years for walking
home with a gram of sugared-down heroin he's got to
put in his arms that night, because if he don't he'll wish
he was dead before morning. Who can figure the law?
The law can't figure the law. You got to take a regular

geography class in criminal law to be able to find out where you can shit anymore without it being a felony."

And the more that was said about the matter of dogs—their dog, Panda, and dogs in general—and the more they discussed the law, the more depressed and ill Bob became. Finally he jumped up and shouted, "It's off, we ain't going to the coast, we ain't going nowhere! Do you know what you have just done to us, Nadine, just by even mentioning dogs in our home?"

"No, I don't, Bob," said Nadine, shaking her head. "What did I do?"

"You just put a thirty-day hex on us, that's what. Right now our luck just flew out the window for thirty days. I wouldn't even cross town with Diane driving now for one month. Have we got a calendar, for chrissakes? Someone mark it off on the calendar, so we'll know when the hex ends, otherwise I'll be moping around here for months, waiting for this thirty-day period to end. What month is it, anyway?"

Rick didn't know what to say, but it was obvious he had to say something. "Jesus, Bob, nobody told us about not saying anything about dogs. How were we supposed to know?"

Bob pulled himself up into his most put-upon, abused manner and answered with, "You know why no one mentioned dogs? I'll tell you why no one mentioned dogs. Because just to have mentioned them would have been a hex itself."

"Well, now that we're on the subject, are there any other sacred subjects or things we're not supposed to do that will affect our future with you?" Rick asked sarcastically.

"As a matter of fact there are a few, and we might as well discuss them right now, being as how we are shut down for thirty days anyway. Hats—if I ever see a hat laying on a bed in this house, the owner won't ever have occasion to wear one again, because I'll beat his head so flat the rain will fall to either side of it. And mirrors. Don't ever look at the back side of a mirror, because when you do you'll affect your future because you're looking at yourself backward. Actually you're looking at your inner self and you don't recognize it because you've never seen that side of yourself before. But anyway, you can put into motion your future that way, and it can be either good or bad. In any case, we just don't want to take the chance.

"And there's cats. A lot of people are frightened of just black cats. I don't distinguish their color, they're all bad. Have you ever noticed how they look at you sometimes, like they're superior to you? Well, that's because they are, they can see what's going to happen to you in your future, and they can readjust your future, especially if you sit on one, step on one's tail, or in any way piss one off. So I just stay clear of the whole mess of them.

"The main thing is just remember the hats. A goddamn hat is the king of them all. It's worth at least fifteen years bad luck, or even death. I'd rather have death myself, because I just couldn't stand no fifteen years bad luck. Jesus, sweet Jesus, can you imagine everything you do going ass backward and uphill for fifteen years?"

Rick and Nadine remained silent, mulling over Bob's latest erratic behavior. But Diane wholly agreed with everything Bob said. She had seen it work out just the way Bob had described time after time. She didn't understand it all, nor did she care to. She just knew that it did affect them and their friends and it was best to avoid the unmentionables whenever possible. So now she said, "Relax, Bob, let's go lay down for a while. You've been on the go for days. This thirty days ain't going to kill us nohow. At least we're lucky that we've got enough stuff to last us that long."

Without another word, Bob turned and left the living room and flopped on the bed, stretching himself out and letting his muscles relax into sagging comfort. Diane followed, turned out the bedroom lights, and silently lay down beside him.

Bob thought it might be nice to drop off to sleep, but then he started thinking about the fate his poor pup met, and then he got back to worrying about hexes. Jesus, he thought, explaining luck to someone who's never had to depend on it every day of his life was a bitch. Hell, he couldn't even figure it out himself. He just knew from years of experience the things to dodge and the signs to look for, like when you jump over a drug counter for a lousy bottle of Percodan because you're too shaky and sick to look for anything better, and then find hidden behind it what you really wanted, the Dilaudid. Now, that was a sign. It was as if whoever managed such things was telling you "Get out there and get it, kid, it's there for the taking and everything's free this week. I'll let you know when your time is up. You'll see the signs."

All you had to do was look for the signs, Bob figured. Some days nothing could go wrong and the dumbest moves got results, and other days nothing went right. They were the ones that were ball breakers, especially if you were suddenly hit with a run of them. It could get mighty sticky out there behind those counters with the sweat running down your ass and your hands shaking so badly you couldn't cop anything without clinking the bottles—if you found them, that is. And you knew it was going to be like this even before you left the apartment, that nothing was going to go down right, that you'd have to fight your way out of every joint you tried to hit. Good God, Bob prayed silently, protect me please from ever having to go out sick and with my luck dragging its heels too. I'm just getting too old for all of that.

Bob felt the warmth and affection of Diane next to him. Little by little, she had snuggled up against her man. Now she said, almost in a whisper, "Don't let it get you down, Bob. Sometimes bad luck can be good luck. I mean, look at all the times we either had a flat or engine trouble and made it to a score late, thinking it was bad luck, only to find out for some reason that it was good luck. You know what I mean?"

Bob turned to fit his body more to the contours of Diane's and said, "That ain't got nothing to do with hexes, though, baby. A hex is a hex and there's nothing good going to come of one. It's just like getting your eyes put out in an automobile crash and then later going on to get a hell of a gig conning suckers out of their money and you can do it because you're blind and people seem to trust blind people more. That ain't good luck, Diane. There ain't nothing that can really come good out of going blind."

"Oh, you and your goddamn hexes," Diane said angrily, rolling away. "Sometimes I believe you're an insane, driveling idiot, Bob Hughes, and right now is one of those times."

Bob winced at Diane's sudden change of mood, but only momentarily. He was used to it. Hell, he was that way himself sometimes.

Thirty days, huh, Bob told himself. Lots of time to do some thinking. His mind wandered back in time, back to the beginning, his first score. He was barely thirteen and it was probably inevitable that he would turn out to be a junkie. His father was a steel-mill worker and a drunk and it was hard to say which of the two finally killed him. Maybe he worked at his job so he could afford to drink, or maybe he drank to be able to contend with the job. Whichever it was, both the drinking and the job made a definite and overwhelming impression on young Bob. He vowed early in life never to follow his father's footsteps. As far as Bob was concerned, hard work killed you and drink made you a fool. They had got his father, but they would never get him.

Bob's family lived in a large industrial town when he was young. The Second World War was in progress and everything was hopping around the clock, so after school and on weekends, Bob hung out on the streets, and in pool rooms and cafés that catered to the local hustlers. This was the time he picked out people to imitate. They happened to be the more honorable types of hustlers and thieves, many of whom were also junkies. Bob didn't stop halfway. He wanted to be like them, and if dope was part of their thing, then it would be part of his thing too.

Drugstore narcotics were in big demand in those days, because most of the European and Asian drug-shipping ports were closed. So drugstores it was. Sometimes the hustlers Bob worshiped were not quite as honorable as they seemed. At least, they didn't feel it was below them to quarterback an impressionable young kid into obtaining what they needed, no matter how chancy the score might prove. What the hell, they thought, if he got caught they wouldn't do much to him. He was only a kid.

Bob did what he was told and learned fast. He became good, too, because he never did just settle for the tried-and-true way. He always looked for a new and easier one. He tried everything, discarding only what proved futile or dangerous. The only thing wrong with his system was that he'd never ask anyone else to do something he wouldn't do himself. So he always played the leading role; and, of course, the odds eventually caught up with him and away he went, to juvenile institutions and, later, the adult ones.

In prison Bob learned never to trust completely another human being, especially with narcotics. He always did his time with grace. He didn't fight it and he didn't let it beat him. Doing time, to Bob, was just a good way to regain his health and build up his veins by lifting weights and getting exercise.

Bob didn't worry about the problems of the outside world. In fact, he never read a newspaper, listened to the radio, or in any way concerned himself with what transpired beyond the prison walls. The prison was his whole world, and its problems, its scandals, and its flow of narcotics were his interests.

During Bob's early incarcerations there were no drug programs. A drug addict was considered lost forever and not worth hassling with. Everybody knew that once a junkie, always a junkie, and that every last one of them would cut their mothers' hearts out for just one more fix.

Later, when the problem mushroomed, especially

among the young, and something had to be done or at
least discussed to please the public, a few loosely run,
half-assed programs were tried in the prisons. But by
then Bob was older and such a confirmed addict that no
one even considered placing him in a rehabilitation program. Bob didn't feel left out, because he didn't think
much of such group plans. He figured the authorities'
first guess probably was right anyway; and that an addict
seldom does change his habits, primarily because he
needs narcotics to function at a level where he no longer
feels insecure or inferior, so that attacks of depression
don't send him around the bend, so he can manipulate
whatever mood or sense of well-being he wishes to at-
tain.

A lot of people don't realize, Bob told himself, just
how lucky they are to be able to go on from day to day,
feeling reasonably good. Oh, they may have a bout of the
flu now and then and they may have to deal with depression when everything goes wrong. But there's just no
way the discomforts the average citizen has to put up
with can compare to the problems the addict has to contend with daily.

Bob often wondered how the fat cats who control narcotics laws would feel if they woke up tomorrow and
found themselves to be black, with little or no education
or training, and with a strong suspicion that nothing
good was ever going to happen to them. Or if maybe they
woke up and found themselves to be a dope-fiend Mexican in the Texas state penitentiary doing a hundred years
for possession of ten dollars' worth of narcotics because
the Texans felt that dope was primarily a Mexican habit
and besides they didn't like Mexicans to begin with. He

wondered how all those big politicians could sit around guzzling alcohol and popping aspirin all night and then proclaim with a straight face that people who can't make it without a crutch, such as the narcotics addicts, should be put away forever.

The whole fucking world was mad, what with a prejudiced majority sanctioning and even demanding that others be prosecuted for doing what they objected to— or were brainwashed into objecting to by slick operators who saw the law as a means to enlarge their fortunes or power base. And even worse than the slick operator was the lowly bureaucrat who didn't have that much to gain. He thought nothing of condemning multitudes of people to confinement in wretched conditions just so he'd always be secure in his job, pushing paper.

And the police were rotten these days, too, as Bob saw it. They were no longer the civil servants of yesteryear, who used to address you as sir, even while writing out a ticket or taking you to jail. No, now they only wanted to scour the gutters for human debris they could collect without offending anyone in high places, and they wanted a say in how their clients were punished. They only spent a few minutes with their victims in the arrest and booking rituals, but they argued that they had first-hand experience with offenders, and that this close contact gave them the insight to condemn them all. But just wait until a cop gets convicted of dealing narcotics or even murdering someone for hire and then other officers are the first to come to his aid. He needed the money, that's why he dealt drugs. His wife was sick and his children were hungry. He had to do something. Jesus, Bob thought, if the public ever began to realize just how weird, kinky, and power hungry most policemen were, it would scare them to death. It seemed like the more they were lacking in any kind of compassion and the more they called for severe punishment, the more likely it was that they were lawbreakers themselves. Bob had seen it proven time after time.

The history of the human race didn't exactly speak well of the participants. Why, not that long ago, in this country no less, people burned other people for witchcraft. Bob often wondered who had gained by it. Someone had, he was sure of that. No one went to all the trouble of promoting such a gruesome business without some gain in mind, even if it was only vengeance for some deeply felt personal pain. As bad as he was—and even in his milder moments, he himself was the first to admit he was no model of Christian virtue—Bob didn't get his kicks from hurting people. He didn't dream up schemes—and then bring them into being with money and influence—to lock up humans in little cages with inadequate or nonexistent sanitary facilities, so they would be driven even more bitter and insane. No, in Bob's mind the real villains were the unthinking bureaucrats, the sadistic police officers, and above all, the politicians.

Crime fighting and punishment: together they constituted a surefire stepping-stone for politicians. It gave them something to get up on a soapbox and rave about. It got their names in the papers. No one had to be smart to learn one brief, to-the-point speech condemning no-good muggers, thieves, and murderers. And it was easy to dispense with the well-meaning, logical, but less ambitious among the political candidates by shouting louder than they could or would and by condemning them, too, for being soft on crime. There wasn't a politician, Bob figured, from Hitler right down to the lowliest mayor in the smallest rural town, who wouldn't starve or even outright hang fifty people for fifty votes. And what made it so easy for them was the fact that they didn't have to face the people they condemned. They didn't see them, so they didn't exist. It was as simple as that. After all, politics was just a game, a game without rules, except possibly one, which was to pick out your most vulnerable adversary and go for the jugular.

While Bob was stretched out on the bed, thus occupied with his thoughts, a five-year-old dark-gray van sat across the street. Inside that cold van were Detectives Gentry and Halamer. Gentry was watching the apartment through a telescope that fit into an ingeniously camouflaged hole in the side of the van. Halamer sipped chilled coffee and bitched. "Why don't we just go on up, plant some stuff on them, and drag them on in? Hell, we got a lot of guys that way."

Gentry drew back from the telescope, blinked a couple of times to clear his vision, and assumed a superior pose. "I'll tell you why," he began. "I don't want to get Bob Hughes on no chickenshit possession beef, and that's all you're going to get on him unless you catch him cold on his way home from a score. And besides, that Bob's different from most of the big-time dealers we plant stuff on. I mean, if you can't get a guy no other way, because he don't ever come within ten miles of the stuff himself and has others handle it for him, well, you just about got to plant some stuff on him to get him. But this is not like that. To begin with, Bob has always got some stuff around someplace. He's got to, hell, he's got to be in that spoon at least six times a day, and he's probably in it twenty. And then there's another thing. Bob just won't sell any stuff. It ain't stuff to him, it's his fucking life. He might give some to a real close friend, or he might trade some off for something else he wants real bad, but he won't take no cash for none, so you're not going to ever get him on a sales. The best we can hope for is a grand theft and a possession with intent to sell. Or if he keeps playing with those matches, maybe an arson beef. I think we scared him off that trip, though. At least he'll be mighty careful about where he lights one off for a while.

"You see, Bob isn't really all that bad a guy. He does have a little class and I've got to respect him, as much as I hate the sonofabitch. And I already told you, he runs in spurts while he follows his luck, and when he's hot he runs like a dog, and when he's cold he'll just lay up in some bolt hole someplace and you'll never see hide or hair of him. I know the sonofabitch. I've been chasing old Bob for fifteen years, and hell, he was a pro back then. I think they got him on his first pharmacy when he was thirteen years old, and what's he now, thirty-three, thirty-five? The guy's been working at his trade for twenty, maybe twenty-five years. He knows what it's all about, believe me. He can actually smell heat. He probably knows we're sitting out here right now and has probably snuck his lawyer in the back way, and will have him sitting up there when you come in to try to lay down a plant on him. I'm telling you, the guy is ingenious. But like I said, he does run in spurts and sometimes he gets to running so hard he don't know when to stop, and I think this may well be one of those times. Hell, he did

just make two real nice scores and he just knows everything's got to be going his way. He'll move again, you
watch. And if he does, we'll be right on his case. And if
we are, we'll get him, because if you can just get Bob in a
drugstore, you got a case, what with all the priors he's
got. I mean, any jury will convict him on little or nothing
just because he's so notorious."

Halamer took another sip of his cold coffee. "Yeah, but
what are we going to do in the meantime, just sit out here
and freeze our fucking balls off? What if we have to wait a
month? I just don't think I could do that. There ought to
be something I could do in the meantime. Maybe I could
get a ladder and sneak up and take a peek in his window
from time to time. I mean, hell, if he's in the spoon
twenty times a day like you say, I ought to be able to catch
him at it sooner or later, and if he's got all those priors,
just my testimony will hang him in front of any jury."

"Well, it's up to you, I won't interfere with whatever
you want to try," Gentry replied. "But just be goddamn
careful. The guy is no fool. I doubt if he would be so
dumb as to fix in front of an uncurtained window, but he
might, being as he's up on the second floor and off the
ground now. You just never know what any of these guys
will do. Just be goddamned careful."

Late at night three days later a knock sounded on the
apartment door. Bob jumped off the bed, got the rest of
the crew to clean up the apartment, and looked out the
peephole in the door. He saw a little old lady standing
out there in a dressing gown and bedroom slippers. She
wasn't familiar, but he could hardly imagine her as part

of the narco force. So finally he opened the door and politely asked her, "What's the problem?"

"Well, I live on the first floor of this building," the little old lady said, "and I've been here for twenty years now. I'm sorry to bother you young folks like this, did I wake you up?"

"No, we were still up." Bob smiled back.

"Well, I don't know what to think, but I was just getting ready to go to bed and I saw this sinister-looking man with a ladder creeping around in the bushes outside. I wonder if you would be so kind as to go out there and look around and see if he's gone. I'm afraid I just wouldn't be able to sleep with one of those crazy sex maniacs running loose in the neighborhood. I didn't call the police because they have so much to do these days, with the crime rate going up and everything, and maybe it'd just be enough if you went out there, because when those sex maniacs know a man is around, it scares them off. They're not very brave, you know."

Bob had the hardest time repressing his laughter. He was glad he wasn't a cat burglar climbing in her window some dark night. Probably get a rolling pin on the skull. But at the same time, he was not amused by what she had seen. He assured her that he would investigate and sent her back to her apartment. Then he sat down on the couch for the longest time while Diane, Nadine, and Rick just stood and watched. Finally he jumped up and said, "Well, they must have followed us when we moved, so I guess we'll just have to teach them a little lesson."

The next morning Bob was up bright and early, studying the surrounding houses. The one next door to the apartment, with the late-fifties red pickup sitting out front, looked promising. And Bob decided it would do just fine when he saw a large, rough-looking man leave for work with his lunchbox under his arm. The guy was no doubt a working stiff and a redneck sonofabitch, Bob figured. He chuckled to himself.

Later that morning, Bob sent Nadine down to the corner grocery for writing paper, envelopes, stamps, and a ball-point pen. He also asked her to copy down the address of the house next door.

When she returned, he wrote a letter to the narcotics division in printed block letters. Then he sent Nadine out again to post it, and retired to the bedroom, where he laid back, waiting for the events to transpire.

"What did you put in that letter, anyway?" Diane asked him.

"I just wrote the narcos and anonymously told them that the reason they could never get Bob Hughes for possession of narcotics was that he had an arrangement with the guy that lived on the north side of him, that they had a thin string running between their houses and that Bob signaled the guy when he wanted some stuff, and that the guy in the other house simply put it on the string and then Bob pulled over what he needed and left the rest in the other house, where they would never find it."

Diane looked at her man as though he had just gone crazy. "Just what good is that going to do? Even if they raid that guy's house they ain't going to find nothing. They ain't even going to find no string. They're going to know they've been tricked and they'll then no doubt enlist the guy's aid, and we'll be in worse shape than ever. They'll be camped right next door instead of across the street."

"Just you wait, honey child. Just you wait," Bob said, flashing his practiced evil grin.

And then he turned to look at the wall and daydream. And they were mighty good daydreams, too, for a man who'd just caught a thirty-day hex, he told himself.

Rick and Nadine just sat in their bedroom and played house and doctor. Nadine liked house better, but Rick, he was hell-bent on being a doctor. Neither of them knew what was going on with Bob. They merely humored him and relaxed. At least they wouldn't be going out for thirty days and that was fine with Nadine. She was feeling a lot better because her stomach wasn't bothering her so much, and she just wanted things to stay the same for a while. Rick was young and impatient and eager to get moving, but as long as they weren't going anywhere, he wouldn't complain, not with Nadine there anyway, not as long as he got to play doctor.

The next morning Bob was standing on the sidewalk in front of the apartment, with a lunch sack in his hand, when the guy next door headed for his red pickup. Bob caught up with him and asked, "Say, pal, you live there?"

The redneck grunted a "yeah" while shifting his lunchbox from one arm to the other. He had several daughters and a guy in his position just never knew when some nut was going to try to hustle one of them off. He had had several dings come right up to the door and ask about his daughters, and he didn't like it one damn bit.

The more Bob watched the guy as he talked, the more he knew his plan was going to work, hex or no hex. So after a little neighborly small talk, like "nice weather we're having," and "that's a real sharp pickup you got there," and other such nonsense, after watching the guy

get more and more suspicious of him and more and
more irritated about being delayed leaving for work, Bob
popped his question. "Say, díd you see that fella creeping around your house last night with that ladder?"

The redneck just stared at Bob, alarm spreading
across his features.

"Yeah, well, I never would have seen the guy neither,"
Bob went on, "but the little old lady that lives here on the
bottom floor, she comes up to our apartment about two
o'clock this morning and she says, 'There's one of them
there sex maniacs creeping around the building with a
ladder in his hands.' So I look out the window, and sure
enough, there the guy is, a big ugly sonofabitch wearing
a long, dark trench coat, and he's standing up on top of
this ladder and he's looking in your upstairs windows.
He had one hand underneath his trench coat and I
couldn't tell what he was doing, but to tell the truth it
looked kind of nasty from where I was watching, if you
know what I mean.

"Anyway, I thought of calling the police, but we don't
have a phone, so I figured, what the hell, it's kind of
embarrassing having some ding like that getting caught
in that kind of a position outside your house. I mean, the
first thing all the neighbors and such are going to think is
what could that guy in that house be doing right out in
daylight, so to speak, to catch the interest of such a nut as
that anyway, you know what I mean? So I figured, I'll just
watch the guy, you know, like if the guy had tried to get
into your house, why, I'd have screamed the house down.
It would have probably frightened him away, and if it
didn't, hell, I'd have come over and helped do whatever I
could. But hell, a guy's got to remember those nuts are

usually strong as bears. I mean, one swat and you're gone, and I got an old lady myself to feed. I can't be laying up in no hospital, and leave her laying up here alone, and besides, what if I'd been wrong? What if it had been that guy's house and he was up there watching his wife or something? It could have got embarrassing as hell, you know?"

The redneck kept nodding, agreeing with everything Bob said, and the more Bob went on, the angrier and redder he became. When Bob was finished with his spiel, the redneck muttered, "I'll shoot the sonofabitch. I'll shoot the sonofabitch right in the balls."

Bob backed up a bit. This was going to go better than he had planned. "Wait a minute," he said. "Hold on a second, mister. I don't want no part of no shooting, and I want you to remember I said so. Jesus, you're going to have the cops involved and everything. You just can't shoot some fella because you don't like what he's doing."

"Watch me," the redneck muttered in hoarse anger. "Just watch me!"

"Now, wait a minute," Bob went on. "I want you to remember when we all have to go to court on this thing, that I warned you against this crazy idea of yours and that I want no part of it. I shouldn't have even told you about the guy. I wish I hadn't. In fact, I think I ought to go right in now, borrow someone's phone, and call the police."

By now the redneck's face was crimson with anger, both at the ladder-carrying creeper and at Bob. "Listen, you little scrawny sonofabitch, if you so much as tell one other person about this matter, let alone call the police, I'll wring your little neck, and when I get done wringing it, I'll tear it off and shit in the goddamn hole!"

"Are you threatening me?" Bob asked.

"No, idiot. I'm promising you!"

Bob turned away and hurried down the sidewalk like he had someplace to go. The redneck went back into his house, no doubt to warn his wife that suspicious characters were roaming around the neighborhood. A few minutes later he emerged, got in his pickup, and drove away. As soon as he was out of sight, Bob ran back to his apartment, slammed the door, and laughed all the way to the bedroom, where he flopped on the bed beside a sleepy, naked Diane.

Across the street in the van, Gentry and Halamer sat in thought. What they had witnessed was unusual, to say the least.

"What do you suppose he had in that paper sack?" Halamer asked. "Do you think it might have been junk?"

"I don't know," Gentry answered. "There's only one thing I'm positive of. It wasn't his goddamn lunch."

"Did you see the way they were talking to each other, all the gestures and such? They got something going, they ain't just casual acquaintances, I could see that."

"Yeah, for a minute there, I thought that big guy was going to jump on Hughes and stomp him into the sidewalk. I sure would have liked to see that."

Halamer looked worried. "Yeah, and Bob should have made another move by now."

"This definitely ain't like him," Gentry agreed.

"Well, if he don't move by tomorrow, I'm going to call off this surveillance. We just can't sit here for a month, and it's liable to take that long before he has to run out and get some more dope. I just wish I knew what was going on."

*   *   *

That night, as Detective Halamer was going on the first
shift, he picked up the letter Bob had sent through the
mail to the central narcotics division office. He read it
through twice and said to himself, "So that's what's going on between those two. What a cozy arrangement. No
wonder we can never catch that sonofabitch with anything. He's always got the neighbors holding it for him,
stringing it across whenever he needs some. Ha, well, I'll
bet you I get that sonofabitch now."

Gentry didn't come to work that evening. He had
picked up a cold sitting in the chilly truck on early-watch
surveillance. So another detective filled in for him on this
particular night. He was a big tough Polack, by the name
of Trousinski, and he hated dope fiends with a passion.
There wasn't anything he'd rather do than strangle a
couple of them every night, and this is what he usually
did. In fact, his nickname was "the Strangler." He'd
clamp his paws around the throats of addicts on the
street to keep them from swallowing whatever they held
in their mouths while some other detective tried to knock
out their teeth so he could look in and see if the dopers
were actually holding anything in there or were just gri-
macing in pain. The Strangler's shins were never quite
healed from the jerks and kicks he received from the
dope fiends he held suspended above the ground. So he
was pleased with the temporary transfer from the streets
to a nice quiet surveillance team. Maybe his shins would
finally get a chance to scab up a bit.

Meanwhile, Bob could hardly contain himself all evening. He kept going to the front window of the darkened
apartment and sliding back the curtains to peer down at

the gray van parked below. And every time he looked out, he'd turn away chuckling. Sometimes it would accelerate into prolonged horselaughs, and he would have the hardest time making it back to the bedroom to again lie beside Diane and annoy her with his insane giggling.

Diane just knew something dire was about to happen. Bob could hardly even fix. He'd strain like hell, find a vein, get the register, and then break into a fit of laughter that would convulse him so much that he would miss when he tried to inject the dope. And then he'd look down at the resulting raised bruise on his arm and just laugh some more.

That wasn't like Bob at all. Diane had never in her life seen Bob carry on so.

As midnight approached, Bob made them all get chairs and sit in the dark, facing the curtained windows. He alone sneaked peeks. "Just wait" was all he would say, and then he'd break into another laughing fit, convincing them all that he had finally gone mad. Even Diane, who had untold faith in her husband, began looking disturbed. And, of course, Nadine wanted no part of it. She wanted to go back into her bedroom and play games with Rick. At least that was more amusing than sitting in front of a window she couldn't even see through. At first, Rick humored Bob because he liked him and respected his judgment. But after a while he got to thinking this had gone too far, and he wondered how much more he could take before he finally jumped up and told Bob to get on with his game, or else he and Nadine were heading back to the bedroom to play doctor.

At midnight, Bob saw Halamer and the Strangler relieve the evening shift, and when he realized who it was, he fell back from the window and rolled across the floor laughing, until it looked as if he were having a fit. He pounded the floor and slobbered at the mouth like a mad dog. Finally he began to quiet down. He was getting weak and his sides hurt so bad that he had to shoot some more dope to get the pain to subside.

Finally, at two in the morning Bob saw the detectives leave their van and cross the street, trying to stay in the shadows. They were carrying something, and Bob knew it just had to be the ladder.

Meanwhile, next door, Buford Honeycut, who hailed from Texas, and who had a wife and two daughters to protect, sat waiting in a rocking chair upstairs in his daughters' bedroom. He waited with a 12-gauge semiautomatic shotgun lying across his knees and a low-wattage dresser lamp casting a dim light out the window. He had five rounds in the gun, all loaded with #8 bird shot. He didn't want to kill the sonofabitch, especially with that yellow-bellied varmint across the way knowing all about the situation. He just wanted to make sure the tom-catting, creeping bastard wasn't ever going to have an excuse to peep into his or anyone else's bedroom window ever again. Hell, he thought, if it was a kid, that would be different. He had done a little peeping himself when he was a kid. But it just wasn't normal for a grown man to be doing it. This didn't sound like no damn kid!

Halamer and the Strangler tiptoed quietly across the lawn. They peered up at the curtained window in Bob's apartment and the light shining through the uncurtained one next door. They held a whispered conference and decided to just take a peek in the uncurtained window.

Carefully they raised the ladder and leaned it against

the side of Buford's house, causing a muffled thump.
Then, as Halamer climbed, the Strangler decided it was
as good a time as any to relieve himself. He had been
holding it for some time now, so while he waited for
Halamer and steadied the ladder with one hand, he used
the other to fish out his privates. And there he stood,
totally unaware that two people were watching him,
never imagining that before much longer many more
would ask, "But what was he doing standing outside that
house with his prick in his hand?"

Buford distinctly heard the muffled thump against the
side of the house. "I'll be a sonofabitch," he muttered,
and then quickly raced down the stairs to the first floor.
He hadn't really expected the sex-mad creeper to show
up tonight. In fact, after dwelling for the better part of
the day on what the little scrawny feller had told him, he
had come to the conclusion that someone had put the
guy up to telling him the story and that it was all a rib,
that whoever had engineered the whole incident would
sit back and laugh at him, sitting up night after night
waiting for the creeper to appear.

After parking his pickup that night, Buford had
dropped in on the little old lady next door and asked her
straight out if there was any truth to the story. She had
confirmed it, but even then, who would figure on the
creeper coming back to the same place night after night?
Anyway, now the question was academic, because the
sonofabitch was back and Buford would be spared all
those nights of sitting up there alone waiting for the guy
to show. And after tonight, by God, Buford told himself
—as he charged down those stairs bristling with energy,
with a taste for blood, with a love of the fray oozing out

his pores, with an almost ecstatic anticipation of the task at hand—after tonight, no one would ever peek in his windows again. Hell, he wouldn't even have to bother drawing the curtains. People would remember this night and regard his place with respect and awe when they passed by. Or so Buford figured, chuckling to himself, on raw-edged nerves, as he looked out a first-floor window and beheld the spectacle of the Strangler standing out there on the grass, with the ladder in one big hand and his privates in the other.

"I'll be a sonofabitch," Buford muttered, calming down somewhat at the sight of a stationary target out in the open. "The bastard couldn't even wait until he got up that ladder to take a good peek."

Buford aimed right at the focus of the Strangler's concentration. *Wham,* the shotgun roared. The Strangler was blown to the ground and the ladder clamped in his hand came with him. Halamer, who had been intently trying to find something of import to look at through that bedroom window, started to swing backward with the ladder, then instinctively let go when it became apparent that things were going to get worse before they got better. He landed on top of the Strangler, in a mess of arms, legs, and ladder rungs.

As soon as Buford fired the first round, Bob, who was crouched on the floor peeking around the drapes, reached up with one hand to flip on the living-room lights while he flung back the curtains with the other. The lights from his apartment lit up the yard between the buildings enough for Buford to see that there was yet another antagonist involved in this fiendish plot against his family.

"I'll be a sonofabitch," he said aloud to himself. "There are two of the slimy bastards out there. They must have taken to teaming up, probably met while they were waiting to see the same psychiatrist."

Wham, the shotgun roared once more. This round caught Halamer right in the rump, and he screamed like a banshee while he groped among the arms of the cursing Strangler and the ladder rungs for his gun.

It must be a goddamn trap, Halamer thought. That crazy dope fiend must have gotten hold of some cocaine and went ringy.

Halamer finally got his pistol out of its holster and looked up at the apartment building. Sure enough, there was Bob and his whole crew standing up there in the window, roaring with laughter as they watched. "Well, they won't laugh for long," Halamer vowed. He aimed in their general direction and fired shot after shot until his weapon was empty and useless.

Diane, Rick, and Nadine dove for the floor when the first shot was fired. Bob just stood there rocking back and forth, giggling insanely. Diane grabbed his legs and tried with all her might to pull him to the floor. But Bob just wouldn't cooperate. There was nothing in this world that was going to frighten him from watching this brilliant display of police efficiency.

Meanwhile, with the crack of the pistol shots, Buford couldn't believe his ears. When it finally did register, he said to himself, "So it's a goddamn sex war they want, huh?"

Wham, wham, wham, the shotgun roared and would have roared some more if he had thought to pocket some extra shells. "But who in hell would have thought it was going to turn out to be a goddamn war?" he repeated many times afterward.

They booked Buford Honeycut that morning on charges of first-degree assault on a police officer in the line of duty.

Buford Honeycut scoffed at the charges. "Line of duty! What kind of duty do you call that, one of them standing in my yard jacking off, and the other one peeking in my daughters' bedroom window, hoping to see something he can tell the other one to excite him some more? So just go ahead and try me. I just hope you try me. When I get through with this police department, there won't be another sex maniac left in it." And then he leered at all the detectives surrounding him as though he were wondering how many of them would have to go.

Needless to say, the prosecutor's office dropped the charges against Buford Honeycut. He is probably the only man in existence to have shot at two detectives five times with a shotgun, been arrested in the morning, and been able to return home that evening in time to catch the dinner-hour news while sitting there cleaning his shotgun.

It didn't take Gentry long to piece together the series of events that had occurred prior to the spectacle in the early morning hours concerning Detectives Halamer and Trousinski, citizens Buford Honeycut and Gwendolyn Flemish, and dope fiends Bob, Diane, Rick, and Nadine. When the whole picture neatly came together like a child's jigsaw puzzle, Gentry sat down with the prosecutor and asked, "Do you think we can get him on a charge of conspiracy to commit a first-degree assault? I know the bastard done it, and it shouldn't be all that hard to prove."

The prosecutor was a nattily dressed middle-aged man. He had his feet up on his desk and the end of a ball-point pen in the corner of his mouth. "I don't know, Gentry," he said. "I sure wouldn't want to try the case. I mean, sure, we can sit here and see how it all transpired, but how in the hell are we ever going to convince a jury that this Bob could predict our police officers' move-ments to the degree he would have had to to enable him to set up such a fiendish plot? I mean, how are we going to convince the jury that Bob could foresee the fact that Detective Trousinski would be standing out there in that yard with his prick in his hand, while the other fool, Halamer, was standing at the top of that ladder looking in the window without any warrant, or without any rea-son other than an anonymous letter? And the one out-standing fact that really kills our case is that little old Flemish woman having brought the fact to the attention of Bob, and then repeating it to Honeycut that there were prowlers lurking about. Now, at this point in the story it's in our favor that this was, in fact, the first time Halamer actually did peek in Honeycut's window. But, good Lord, try convincing a jury of that! They'd think, hell, if he got caught doing it once illegally, who says he might not have done it before. No, Gentry, I don't think I want to waste my time with a case like that."

Next, Gentry went to see the chief. As he entered his office door, the chief looked up, grimaced, and asked, "Just what was that fool doing out there with his prick in his hand? Was it some new kind of undercover opera-tion? You got them boys of yours trying to imitate the sexually maladjusted now, so that you can get a look in a building before you enter it? Was that the play?"

Gentry shook his head and cleared his throat excessively. Finally he stated, "You know how it is, Chief, out on those surveillance teams. There's usually nothing to do but sit around and sip coffee, and if you do enough of that, pretty soon you're going to have to find a place to urinate. Well, obviously, Trousinski thought that would be a pretty good spot. Hell, he was up off from the street and almost into the bushes at the side of that house. You can't hardly blame him. He didn't know he'd been set up. Hell, it could have happened to both of us a thousand times."

"Yeah, but it didn't, and it did happen to him, so what are you going to do now?"

"About Trousinski or about Hughes?"

"About Hughes. I know what you're going to do about Trousinski. You're going to have to stand around rest rooms for the rest of your life blocking for him while he relieves himself, so no one else will get a chance to see the damage a 12-gauge shotgun can do to a man's penis at close range."

"Well, Chief, I've been giving that some thought."

"I'll just bet you have. What did the prosecutor say?"

"He said he didn't want any part of it. So I thought, maybe, we just might get rid of that sonofabitch Hughes forever."

"Oh yeah? Well, what do you aim on doing with the rest of them? Seems to me like you're going to have to dig a pretty deep hole to bury all of them. And how are you ever going to catch that little punk without his whole crew along? He don't move alone, not very often, he don't. Besides, I don't much care for the smell of it. Why don't you just scare him off, hint around just what the Strangler and Halamer are going to do to him once they get out of the hospital? Give him the idea that you're looking out for your officers' welfare, that you don't want to see them get into any trouble and that's why you're warning him off. Shit, maybe the sonofabitch will leave town and never come back again. Can you imagine how peaceful this city would seem without Bob Hughes and his crew? Hell, it would be worth losing Trousinski's prick. In fact, I think it's a hell of a deal. Also, you can promote that prickless bastard to the next grade and get him an office job, maybe in the jail or somewhere. And I want that ignoramus Halamer demoted all the way to the bottom of the ladder, and I don't ever want to see him wearing anything but blue ever again. Traffic—transfer him to traffic. That's so bogged up now, he couldn't possibly disrupt anything down there."

Gentry left the chief's office, deciding that a direct confrontation with Hughes was in order. When he rang the bell at Bob's door, the whole crew was involved in packing up their belongings.

Bob went to the peephole, sighted Gentry, and shouted through the door, "You got a warrant?"

"No, Bob, I haven't got a warrant," Gentry shouted back in his most civil voice. "All I want to do is talk to you for a moment about the fracas that happened outside your apartment last night."

"We told the investigating officers all we knew about that," Bob shouted back, "and we haven't got anything further to add."

Gentry shuffled from one foot to the other. His face

began to get red, and for the first time in years, his hands began shaking uncontrollably. "You little punk," he raved, "are you going to open this door or am I going to have to kick it in?"

"I just hope you kick it in," Bob answered nastily. "We got a block watchers' cooperative thing going now to protect us from sex-maniac policemen, and Buford Honeycut is the elected president and sole enforcer. You just kick that door in, buster, and I'll pull my little string and over will stomp big, bad old Buford with his little old shotgun. You think I'm jiving, just kick the door in. I just hope you do, and if you don't have your prick in your hand when he shoots you, you will before the rest of your buddies get here, you can bet your three-yard-wide ass on that."

Gentry stepped away from the peephole and looked at the ceiling while he slowly counted to ten. When he was done, he considered what Bob had said and how much truth there was likely to be in it, and he decided there just might be something to it. So instead of forcing the matter, he began talking through the door. "Bob, the reason I came down here was to warn you. Halamer and Trousinski, they know how you set them up, Bob. And I can honestly say that they are anything but happy about the matter. In fact, to say the least, I feel they have murder in their hearts, and Bob, I'm not warning you because I have any love for you. The good Lord knows I wouldn't even try to tell that lie. The thing is, though, that I just hate to see my two officers get into any more trouble over this matter, if you know what I mean? Oh, we could probably smooth it out in the end and it would no doubt prove to be an accidental shooting, or one where my officers just didn't have any other choice. But Bob, why go through all of that? I mean, I know you don't want to get shot and hurt or maybe killed, and I know I don't want to see it happen either. So why don't you just leave town? Why don't you just go out along the highways and byways of this great, grand country of ours until you find a nice spot to settle down, a place where they don't have tough cops like Halamer and Trousinski, a place that has narcotics drawers just brimming to the top with all kinds of goodies just laying there waiting for you to take them? Can you hear me, Bob? Now, what do you think of a move like that?"

"Fuck you, Gentry. I won the goddamn war, not you. Who are you to dictate the terms? Before I'm through, there won't be a cop left in the city with a prick, or balls neither. I'm telling you this because I always had a soft spot in my heart for you, Gentry. The good Lord knows I'm not lying. Why don't you go find you a small-town police department where you can just step in as chief, where you won't have to put up with any real criminals, where all you've got to worry about is the usual Saturday-night drunks and the kids on Halloween? That would suit you better, Gentry. You can't win at this game. You're just too goddamn dumb."

If there was anything Detective Gentry liked it was a good debate, so instead of getting him more excited, Bob's arguing actually settled him down. "You know what, Bob? You don't even know what a goddamn war is. So you think you won the war, huh? Ha, you didn't even win a minor skirmish. All you did was come out on top in a minor fray. Hell, it will all be forgotten about in a month's time, just like your demise, Bob. Oh, yes, we might have to explain it away for a few days, but sooner or later everyone's going to forget that you ever existed. That is, all but the pharmacists. They'll probably hold an annual ball on the eve of your death for the next twenty years."

"Fuck you, Gentry. I just wish that had been you out there with your prick in your hand. I was just praying that it would be you, you ball-less bastard."

Gentry left, slowly walking away down the hall, thinking that you just couldn't talk to dumb bunnies like Bob. When you tried, when you made an effort to be nice to them, they figured you were getting soft and tried to take advantage of you. Step on them hard, and keep the pressure on—that was the thing to do, the only thing the dumb bastards understood.

As soon as it was obvious that Gentry was gone, Nadine asked Bob, "How come you always talk so nasty to those cops? Maybe he was telling the truth. Maybe he was trying to help us."

Bob shot back a look of pure disgust. "Shit," he said, "whoever heard of a cop helping someone? That crap went out with the forties. They don't even try to keep up that image of themselves anymore. You know what, I talked to a cop nice and respectful once and you know what he did?"

"What?" asked a subdued Nadine.

"He kicked me in the kneecap, that's what the bastard done."

"Well, what do they do when you talk nasty to them?"

"They kick me in the kneecap then, too, but at least then I'm expecting it. You can't ever show any weakness to a chickenshit cop, because then they'll just know they're beginning to get to you, and then they'll never let up, because they think they came so close that one time. No, Nadine, there's a regular goddamn war going on out there, even if you've never taken the time to notice. And it's between the haves and the have-nots. Well, I ain't got nothing to do with it. I'm actually a neutral, and both sides know this, so both sides take this for a weakness in me, because I'm not politically involved with either faction. I'm a goddamn thief, been one all my life—that and a dope fiend—and I haven't got any time for all that political crap. I got to hustle just to get down with my thing, and both those sides want to crowd me, because I do so good and they do so bad. Fuck them, I ain't giving any of them an inch. Oh, we're going to leave town all right, but only because I think it's the smart thing to do. Diane and I haven't been cross-roading in years. Those pharmacies out there in the sticks ought to be fat-fat, and these here in town are getting double tough. We should have gotten out months ago. I knew it then and I know it now, so just don't think any two chickenshit cops are running us out of town, because they ain't. Just get done with that packing, because I want to be out of here just as soon as it gets dark."

The move out of the apartment was made in a series of departures. Diane had to get all the narcotics together, put aside some that they would be taking with them, and then package the rest in individual bags and suitcases that would be sent ahead by Greyhound, addressed to various stops on their route, so they could rendezvous with the drugs as they needed them. Bob had theories about traveling across the country, or cross-roading as he called it, and sending ahead needed drugs was part of it. One just could not be caught heading across the country with a whole carload of narcotics, so they only took along what they could afford to throw away. Should any law-enforcement officer attempt to stop them, that is what they would do. They always had a hole punched through the floorboards of their car, and when the flashing red light became a reality, they merely pulled back the floor mat and proceeded to dump whatever they had down the hole as the driver stalled, keeping the car moving until it all was gone.

But then came the scramble for the next rendezvous, because at best, the crew had only eight hours before withdrawal hit to the point that no one could drive. Sometimes, at this point, they would just pull into the nearest hospital and lay their cards on the table, telling the doctors there just what the problem was. Sometimes they'd find sympathy and a shot that would get them down the road, and sometimes they'd get nothing but a police escort out of town, along with a warning never to return.

PART II

Two days later, Bob, Diane, Rick, and Nadine registered at a motel in the largest city of the adjoining state. They all fixed numerous times, trying for a state of euphoria that didn't have them exactly lying full-length on the floor, but left them feeling that they didn't much care if they had been.

Bob had been at the speed bag again and was pacing the floor while holding a telephone book and rattling off various names of pharmacies, hospitals, and veterinarians.

Diane was sprawled in an overstuffed chair. She rubbed her legs and thighs, wet her lips, trembled occasionally, and sighed often as though that were the only way she could keep breathing, while her eyes followed Bob back and forth across the room.

Rick was lounging on the room's only couch, with his

head cradled in Nadine's lap. His eyes were closed and his mind was a thousand miles away. Every once in a while Bob's voice would break its way into his thoughts, and at those times, he would mutter, "Oh, my God." And before that short sentence was out, his mind would be off and racing along other corridors not even remotely related to drugs, this place, or the people around him.

Nadine just sat there and tried to put it all together—her life, her future, her man, and the way everything was going. And no matter how it all went together, it came out zero for all of them. It was like trying to bail out the ocean with a tomato-soup can. The more you bailed, the more immense the waves seemed to grow. And the worst part of it was, you knew you could never win. You even went into this game knowing you couldn't win, so what kind of a game was that? Who played games you could not win? *Lots of people,* Nadine answered herself, *I guess lots of people do.*

"Okay," Bob finally announced. "Let's get off our duffs and out on the road. We ain't going to find no morphine hanging off the fir trees. We got to get out there and run some down. Diane, you pick out some doctors and try putting the old sexy, pee-pee act on them. Rick and Nadine, you come along with me. We got to find out first just what poison shops in this town are holding."

Bob, Rick, and Nadine took the car and checked out the pharmacies downtown. It went like this: Nadine would enter the store and pretend to browse around the pharmacy counter. Rick would also walk in and hang around the drug counter, but at a different spot so he could see from a different angle and perhaps notice something that Nadine might miss. Meanwhile Bob would step into a phone booth down the street, call the pharmacist, and ask, "Say, I've got a one-milligram Dilaudid prescription and I've been all over town trying to find some. Could you possibly fill this prescription for me?"

The whole point of this operation was to get the pharmacist to look in his narcotics stash to see if he had any one-milligram Dilaudid tablets (thereby showing the crew just where the stash was), to find out whether or not the pharmacy in question even stocked Dilaudid in any form, and to discover just what the attitude of the pharmacist was concerning Dilaudid, narcotics prescriptions, and narcotics in general.

At one place, Nadine watched the pharmacist talking to Bob on the phone change from a smiling, good-natured type to a frowning, snarling, no-nonsense one. "No, we don't have any Dilaudid in any form. We haven't carried any of that crap in years, so don't bug us anymore."

"What was that all about?" an inquisitive clerk asked the pharmacist after he slammed down the phone.

"Oh, one of those goddamn dope fiends again, asking if we stock one-milligram Dilaudid."

"Dilaudid, good Lord, I haven't seen a bottle of that around in years. We don't even have any, do we?"

"No, I don't stock the stuff anymore. I used to, but those crazy dope fiends about drove me crazy over them. All day long they were pestering me for broken-up tablets, trying to push off phony prescriptions on me, and at night they crashed through my front door, through the back door, through the roof; I expected any goddamn minute to find one come crawling down the chimney."

Nadine and Rick turned away in disgust. As they sauntered out the door, the pharmacist and his clerk followed their movements. When they were gone, the pharmacist let out a sigh of relief and told the clerk, "That was a couple of them right there, I'd bet my bottom dollar on it. Did you see the way they stood around trying to look so innocent and prim? Yeah, that was a couple of the bastards. They run in packs just like wolves, and don't let them think you've got a narcotic drug left on the shelf or they'll pester you until they get it. They just don't know when to give up. They'll come into your store in droves and one of the bastards will actually hold you, just wrap his arms around you and hold you while the others in his pack rip off your shelves. They're like a horde of locusts. There isn't anything you can do once they find out you're stocking what they are after."

"Why don't you call the police?" asked the baffled clerk.

"Police? You ever try to work one of these counters with a goddamn fat-assed cop crouching on the floor by your counter all day long and jumping up every few minutes to sneak around and take pictures of your customers? Hell, I'd rather put up with the dope fiends. At least what they steal isn't worth much monetarily. The goddamn cops will steal you blind, and they'll take stuff that's worth a damn sight more, like penicillin and birth-control pills. God, how they like those birth-control pills. No, no more cops for me."

As Nadine and Rick approached Bob on the sidewalk, they slowly shook their heads in unison. Bob grinned and said, "Don't look so glum. The bastard's holding, all right."

"I don't know, Bob," Nadine responded. "After you called, the clerk asked the pharmacist what it was all about and he said it was some dope fiend inquiring about Dilaudid and then the clerk said, 'Hell, I haven't seen any of that stuff in years.' "

"Oh, yeah, well they were just putting the shuck on you, because I know the bastards had Dilaudid in there not too awfully long ago. And besides, they wouldn't have gotten so paranoid if they weren't holding. They wouldn't have been so scared and nasty. They're holding, all right, for their hometown customers. You watch, I'll show you one of these days."

The rest of the pharmacies went pretty much the same way, and all it proved to Bob was that this town had obviously been worked thoroughly in the not too distant past.

Diane spent the morning calling doctors and trying to make appointments for the afternoon, the next morning, or at the latest, the next afternoon. She made a few appointments, and they went about like this:

She would enter the outer office and approach the secretary. "I have an appointment to see Dr. Clark at one thirty. Will he have time to see me then?"

"Yes, I believe so. Is this your first appointment with Dr. Clark?"

"Yes, it is."

"I see. Will you please fill out this personal history form?"

"Thank you, I will."

Diane would then begin filling out the form, and where

it asked for a description of her immediate medical problem, she would write "kidney pain."

Finally the secretary would motion to her and say, "You may enter, Diane. Go through this door, follow the hallway along to the second door on your right. Enter that door and wait for the doctor. While you are waiting, you might as well undress and put on the white gown you'll find draped across the stool in the room."

The first thing Diane did after entering the examination room was thoroughly shake down all the drawers and cabinets, looking for prescription blanks. This time she couldn't find any. Next she removed all her clothes, folded them, and placed them in a pile on one of the cabinets. Then she took a small safety pin out of her purse, and pinned it low, inside the hem of her white gown. After that, there was nothing to do but sit on the stool and practice her dire-pain looks, checking the results in the glass of one of the medical cabinets, and then laugh to herself.

Several minutes later a smiling, professional, middle-aged man opened the door and entered with a plain-looking young nurse on his heels. "And how are you today? This is your first visit with us, isn't it?" the doctor asked, while studying the personal-history card Diane had filled out.

Diane put on her most pained expression, lifted her gown to her waist, pointed between her legs, and said, "I hurt right here sometimes, and back here all the time." And then she pointed to her lower back, where someone had told her the kidneys were located.

"Hmm, I see," said the doctor. "And just how long has this been bothering you?"

"Well, you see, it used to bother me about a year ago, and I went to the doctor and he gave me some pills, codeine I think they was, and boy, they really made me sick, made me swell up all over. But then he gave me some little tiny white ones, laudid, or something like that, and they helped kill the pain. And then he gave me some other ones that made me pee blue, and after I took both of them for a while the pain went away, and I haven't been bothered since until last week and then it started all over again. I thought if I just held out it might go away, and I've suffered along with it as best I could, but I just can't stand the pain no longer, especially when it goes down to my pee pee. Oh, my God, does it ever hurt then. I just can't stand it any longer. Do you think this is a serious ailment, doctor? Do you think I'll be bothered with it all the rest of my life? My mother used to have this same thing before she died."

And then Diane would sniffle a couple of times and look as if she were going to break down in tears at any moment.

"There, there now, just stand up here and let me feel your back. Hmm, does it hurt there? There? There? How about there?"

The nurse hovered around like a hummingbird looking for a place to land while she waited to take notes of significance. And Diane moaned and groaned every time the doctor pressed his fingers into any area of the back where she supposed her kidneys were.

"Hmm," said the doctor. "You've got kidney stones. It's nothing really serious, but it can get painful at times. My best suggestion to you is to eat a lot of hard Christmas candy. Don't chew it up, though, suck it slowly. That way the saliva coming from your glands will go down to your stomach and help dissolve those little stones, which are actually calcium deposits and granules of salt. Don't eat any more salt than you have to, either. Now, I'll just send you down the hall to the lavatory with the nurse and she'll give you a bottle. We want you to urinate in it, so try to give us enough to send to the lab for analysis. I won't give you a prescription right now, but you come back in the morning, say, around eleven. I'm sure the lab report will be in by then, and we'll know exactly what we're up against and then I'll fix you right up."

"Thank you, doctor," said Diane, smiling at him while still holding to her contortions of pain.

Then she followed the nurse to the lavatory, took the small bottle, entered a booth, and sat on the toilet seat. Taking the safety pin from the gown, she pricked her finger, let two drops of blood fall into the bottle, and then filled the bottle with urine as requested. Blood in the urine, a sign of kidney stones, would get Diane her prescription for sixty one-thirty-second grains of Dilaudid the next morning. She would also get a prescription for some pills to help dissolve the stones, which she would blithely throw away.

That evening, they all returned to the motel. "How'd you do?" Bob asked Diane.

"Oh, so-so, you know how it goes. I'll reap the harvest on three pers in the morning. Should come home with one hundred and eighty thirty-seconds."

"Oh yeah? Hell, that ain't bad. The way those druggists were shying away from us today, you'd have thought this town had been worked like a Mexican whore. Did you hear that, Rick? Diane's doing all right."

Diane grinned as Bob spoke, and asked in her most pleading manner, "Bob, do I got to keep on hustling those goddamn doctors? You know how I hate all that hassle. Why can't we just heel, crash, and roof pharmacies? I hate those damn doctors, and all that waiting around those funky offices."

"Goddamnit, Diane," Bob said, shaking his head in annoyance. "You know it all goes together. We got to have those prescriptions to be able to find out for sure just which pharmacies are holding, to have an excuse to visit those hospital pharmacies so we can look them over. And besides, the few you pick up always seem to come in handy. It don't matter how much dope you got today, it's always going to be hell tomorrow. So you got to keep looking ahead. Hell, I never promised you no rose garden. Whoever told you being a dope fiend was the easy life? Hell, it's goddamn hard work, that's what it is. Nothing but hard work from daylight to dark. Ain't no construction stiff, working two shifts a day, that puts out more just plain hard work and takes more stress and strain than us, and you know it. And once you get lazy, you're dead. You might as well pick up a pistol and put a hole right through your head, because a lazy dope fiend, he ain't got no place to roost except in prison, or on his back selling ass for whatever he can get. How'd you like to do that? Spend all night in some crummy whorehouse going down on dirty old men to get enough money to get well in the morning? You think you'd like that better? Hell, I can get you all a job laying on your back if you want one. Me, I'll work for a living, I'll take the doctors and pharmacists. At least if one does corner you and the only way you can get out is by going down on him, chances are he'll be clean."

Bob picked up his chin and tugged at his belt and went to the window and looked out on the street. Hell, to run a crew you got to know what you're doing, he told himself. Like picking a crew to begin with, you gotta have judgment. You got to know when to lay down the law, because maybe they'll start slipping and you can't let them do that or they'll take you right with them. You just got to know when they need whipping into shape, or if they're just sort of plugging along, making it from one day to the next, you got to know how to inspire them. Running a crew, it's not a job just any fool could fill. Hell, there was no two ways about it—you just had to be a combination of straw-boss foreman and Freudian psychologist, with a little slapstick comedian thrown in every once in a while to keep things loose. You had to be a leader of men, and women, too, because, like now, even the old lady can get to hanging her head and needing to be picked up, to keep bucking odds that no Jimmy the Greek would ever let his nickel get near. You've got to be damn good, Bob told himself, one step ahead of the rest of the world at all times. Somewhere in the back of his mind, he felt a twinge of yearning for respect from that world, a longing for just a shade of legitimacy, a little recognition from somebody other than the fucking cops for his skills and ideas, a cushion to lean on in old age, a fifty-year pin, something! But he knew the only thing he was likely to get was a bullet through the heart.

The next morning, Bob and Rick went downtown and rented a small, red Toyota pickup truck. This was in line with Bob's theory that they needed a second car anyway, and one with this state's license plates. Also, the small red pickup would blend into the community, Bob figured, after carefully screening the vehicles around town. The loud color was so obvious it might throw off the heat, and added to the fact that there were plenty of such vehicles around, it could prove more than a little confusing to anyone trying to keep track of their movements.

That evening, Diane felt ill and took to bed. But Bob was on the go again and wanted to do something, even if it was wrong. So he got Nadine and Rick in the mood to join him, and they climbed in the pickup and headed for the heart of the city. On the way, Bob gave his usual lectures on drug thefts and thefts in general. Tonight's theme was that there is always something you can steal, except that sometimes it is so obvious that it escapes the casual observer.

They parked the pickup and roamed the streets, examining the closed businesses. Every now and then they'd come upon an open café or bar, and they never passed one without entering, if only for a moment, and ordering something, even if they didn't particularly want it, so they would look like a trio out for a good time rather than a band of thieves casing the town.

They had been on the streets about an hour when they came to the first drugstore they had visited that morning. They walked by, but then Bob pulled up and asked excitedly, "Did you see that?"

"What?" said Rick, and he and Nadine turned back to see what they had missed. All they could see was a darkened pharmacy. Nothing to get excited about, hell, they had passed by a dozen of them already tonight.

"The transoms, didn't you guys see the open transoms? Wow, what a bird's nest on the ground, and you guys never even saw it. What was I just telling you, you got to keep your eyes open, you got to look. There's stuff just laying out, waiting for you to steal if you only got eyes and the good sense God gave you to see it with. And that nasty-assed bastard pharmacist saying, 'No, we don't have no Dilaudid, haven't stocked that crap in years.' Well, well, we'll just see if that bastard wasn't lying through his teeth or not, right this goddamn minute. Rick, you go back to the pickup and get that small bar I shoved under the front seat. Nadine and I will walk around a bit and see what-all is happening on this street. See if there's any drunks or couples sitting around in any of these cars parked along here."

Rick left and Bob and Nadine sauntered along, checking the cars. Nadine asked Bob, "How are you going to do it?" Her voice cracked, revealing her growing nervousness.

"Well, I'll tell you what, baby. When Rick comes back I'll just show you. Ain't going to be nothing to it. You just get that bar when Rick brings it and stick it under your coat. But be ready to hand it to me at a moment's notice, because I don't want to get trapped in that joint if they do have an alarm. I don't think they do, because I can't see one, but you never know in this day and age and that damn joint looks almost too good to be true, all darkened like it is. I haven't seen such a good thing since I was a kid, and that was a good many years ago."

Presently, Rick returned, puffing, with the bar under his jacket. At Bob's nod, he handed it over and Bob passed it on to Nadine.

"Okay, Rick, here's the play. We get the traffic right

first, then we move over in front of those open transoms. You cup your hands, I stick my foot in, you lift, up I go. I'll be pulling and you'll be lifting, so I'll go fast. Now, just before I slide over that damn windowsill, get out of the way, because then Nadine has to move up so she can hand me that bar right at the last minute, just as my hand is going over and down. You both got all that?"

Nadine and Rick nodded.

"Okay, then, I'll scramble for the back end of the store. You both run around to the alley entrance, because if at all possible, that's where I'll be exiting from. And then we'll just amble on over to the truck. It's just parked on the next street, isn't it, Rick? Just opposite from where we are standing now?"

"Yeah," said Rick.

"Good, that's fine. We can probably pass right across that parking lot back there and make our way to the pickup. Okay, everybody got their thing down?"

Again they nodded. Bob looked furtively up and down the street, until it was clear. "Okay, this is it," he said.

Bob and Rick moved fast, stepping up under the pharmacy's entrance and Rick lifting while Bob pulled. Nadine seemed to be almost in a trance as she kept one eye on them and one on the street. It was still quiet. Bob almost flew through the open transom, and as his legs slid over the edge, his one gloved hand remained grasping out over the edge. Nadine reacted by handing him the pry bar, and Bob dropped to the floor. He whirled and raced along the shelves until he came to a locked door leading to a back room. With a deft movement, Bob sprung the door in a matter of seconds. Now he was in an area that was divided into two sections. The first section was made of rough, dirty, aged wood. Two safes sat against one wall. One was nothing more than a square firebox and the other was a plug-type, round door, commonly known as a money chest. Also in this part of the back room was the alley entrance, which had a huge, sliding wooden door, secured on the inside by a padlock on a cheap hasp. Bob tore it off quickly to ensure his exit should he trip an alarm.

Next he turned to the other section of the back room. That was the pharmacy, and it was built of aluminum and glass. Bob attacked a small sliding door and entered, moving quickly along the shelves of pills and salves. Halfway along the main counter he found the locked drawer. It wasn't too large, but when he sprung it open, he found that it was heaped to the brim with small bottles of different colors and design, but which were similar in one respect. They each had a purple federal tax stamp on the cap. Bob grinned as he grabbed the whole drawer and ran for the alley exit. He slid open the rear door and found Rick and Nadine waiting. He handed the drawer to Nadine, saying, "Take this, baby, and put it in the truck. You, Rick, step inside here a moment. I want you to look at these two safes."

Rick stepped into the building and Bob turned to watch Nadine cross the parking lot. She walked only a few steps, then started to run, clutching the drawer to her abdomen like some cigarette girl with a tray of the finest Turkish blend. She ran so hard, the small bottles jostled to the point that she sounded not unlike the early morning milk truck just beginning its delivery. When she reached the truck, she hesitated beside the bed, and as she stood there, Bob imagined he could actually see the wheels of thought turning in her cute little head.

Nadine started to lower the whole drawer into the bed, then thought better of it and let it rest on the bed's side panel momentarily while she opened the truck's door on the driver's side. Then she grabbed the drawer, swung it backward as far as her arms would arc, and then brought it forward as if she were a fishwife emptying a pan of water, spilling the bottles all over the seat and floor of the truck.

Bob couldn't believe what he was seeing. He yelled at Rick to forget about the safes. Rick emerged from the building, closed the alley door, and turned, just in time to see Nadine bend down with the empty drawer between her legs, straighten up and flip the drawer up and over her head. It sailed into the air, spun around a couple of times, and landed in the street a few parking meters away.

Rick and Bob took off running toward Nadine and the pickup. About this time a small gray Volkswagen rounded a corner and slowed down near the drawer, seemingly studying it momentarily. Then it drove on, but another car was coming as Bob and Rick reached the badly shaken Nadine. They quickly pushed her into the pickup and Bob pulled away, sitting on a pile of bottles, for once saying nothing.

Bob turned corner after corner. He'd go straight ahead for a couple of blocks, then circle a block and head off in another direction. Finally he found what he wanted, a semiresidential district. He stopped at the first house with enough bushes to conceal Nadine and the bottles.

"Okay," he said, "let's get all these bottles together, and I mean every one, put them in a sack and you, Nadine, you take that sack and walk, don't run, over to those bushes alongside that house and wait for us while we go back and get that damn drawer and clean it up. You didn't have any gloves on, baby, and that clean cream drawer is going to have nothing but your fingerprints all over it, and baby, unless we get back and get that drawer and wipe them off, the chances are you're going to get to see the inside of the women's prison here in this fine state, because you're going to have the damndest prima-facie case against you that I ever heard tell of."

They worked in silence and it only took them a few moments to pick up all the bottles. Not one of the bottles had broken, which was almost unbelievable. Bob just knew he was going to have to lie down on the floor of that truck and scoop out broken glass and then search for the small tablets.

Nadine got out and, holding the sack high in her arms like any normal shopper, walked to the bushes as Bob and Rick headed back toward the pharmacy. Bob breathed a sigh of relief when he saw the drawer sitting right where Nadine had tossed it. Rick jumped out, grabbed it, jumped back in, and Bob took off with a jerk, turning corners again to try to duplicate their previous route. They eventually found a huddled, shaking Nadine and hustled her into the truck, while at the same time throwing out the carefully wiped drawer.

As soon as they returned to the motel, Diane got out of bed and came in to watch them go through the bag of narcotics. But Nadine didn't stay. She marched off to her bedroom with a bowed head and then slammed the door shut.

"What's that all about?" Diane asked. "You been making a pass at her, Bob?"

Bob shook his head and pawed through the pile of small bottles. Presently he came up with a small one with a blue label. "I'll be goddamned," he said.

"What is it, Bob, what did you find?"

"Powdered Dilaudid, that's what. A whole goddamn one-eighth-ounce bottle of powdered D. And there should be another partially filled bottle here somewhere."

He spread them all out on the coffee table and separated them into different categories.

"You know what this bottle is worth, Rick?" Bob asked, holding up something that was no larger than a nail-polish bottle.

Rick studied the bottle awhile and shook his head.

"Well, I'll tell you what it's worth. It's worth a goddamn fortune, at least a small fortune. That there bottle's got eight hundred and forty some-odd sixteenths in it, and at ten dollars a sixteenth, that comes to around eight thousand four hundred dollars' worth of the best goddamn dope money can buy. Yep, that there little bottle will probably last us three for a week. Hot dog, what a find! I guess we must have outrun that hex we had on us. I sure am glad we started cross-roading, ain't you, Diane?"

And with that he took a willing Diane in his arms and whirled her around the room as she squealed and shrieked in delight.

In the bedroom, Nadine sat on the edge of the bed, her

coat still on and the tears slowly coursing down her cheeks. The more she listened to them out there, the more unhappy she became. It was almost as if their happiness was her undoing, she thought.

After the three had fixed, Bob announced, "Okay, pards. I'll show you how we'll hide this stuff in these motels. Diane, get a chair and put it in the closet, open up that trap door to the attic, and I'll push you on up through. You cross over a couple of these units and stash the stuff in the insulation over somebody else's room."

When the stash was put away, Bob turned to Rick. "Why don't you go on in and fix up your old lady. Tell her us three will be going out for a couple of hours. Hell, we might as well go over and see how that hospital we looked at this morning looks at night. Maybe we can just creep the sonofabitch. We're running hot tonight, and I ain't giving it up until it begins to look like everything is going to go wrong."

Rick entered the bedroom and stood awhile just inside the door, watching Nadine. She still sat on the bed with her coat on and head lowered.

"Buck up, baby. So you muffed it, everyone does that once in a while. It came out all right and that's what counts. Here, let me fix you up a couple of these sixteenths. You'll feel just fine then. We're going to go out again, but don't worry, we'll be back soon. You just try to get some sleep."

Nadine raised her tear-stained face. "What did that sonofabitch say about me?"

"Baby, he didn't say anything," Rick said, smiling. "Not one word. Diane doesn't even know anything about it."

"But he isn't going to take me along anymore, is that it? And one day you all will just drop me off on a corner and tell me to do such and such and I'll come back and wait and wait and you'll never show up. You'll be gone to the next town, and I'll just have to make do with what I can. I'll get sick and not have anyplace to go, no one to help me, no one to turn to, and you guys will just laugh as you drive out of town down the highway, you'll laugh about how I ran, how I lost my nerve and ran. I know you will, goddamnit."

And then her voice broke into sobs and the trail of tears became a flood.

Rick knelt beside the bed and held her. "Baby, we ain't going to leave you standing on no corner. We ain't leaving you anyplace. You're mine, baby. I'm not leaving you. If they even suggest something like that, which they won't, I'd leave them and go off with you, and you know it. So buck up, now, Nadine. And you'll work with us again. Bob is no doubt leaving you home tonight because he knows you're feeling bad. You watch. Tomorrow we'll be out on the streets again like nothing ever happened. I'll bet you he never ever mentions it to you again. He knows how bad you feel about the whole thing."

"To hell with that sonofabitch and his hexes and all his funny little stunts. It wasn't my fault we had to leave the coast. That was his fault. I didn't set up no policeman. He did. Why can't we just go off on our own? We can do the same things they do, and without them. The goddamn hogs. We wouldn't have to do it so often. We could make it good, Rick. I know we could."

"Now, baby, you just take it easy. We got us a good thing going. Why break it up? Things are going all right.

You're just upset tonight. You just wait until tomorrow. You'll see things in a different light then and everything will be fine."

"No, Rick, they're not going to be fine. I just can't stand their superior ways and all that crap about hexes. You don't believe that stuff, do you?"

"Hell, I don't know, Nadine. What difference does it make, anyway? It's their thing. I guess if they want to believe in hexes, they're entitled to. You know, sometimes a thing works for some people just because they believe in it so much. And what the hell, all we got to watch for is not talking about pets in their presence and not leaving any hats on any bed. Hell, there's nothing hard about that."

"Well, I'm just going to prove to all of you that there isn't anything to any of that stuff."

Nadine marched straight to the closet and promptly took out one of her hats. She determinedly flipped it onto the bed and then asked Rick, "Do you think it will make any difference that I'm using a woman's hat instead of a man's?"

Rick shook his head slowly. "I wish you hadn't have done that, Nadine. It really isn't fair. I mean, you can do whatever you want to change our lives, but why do you want to mess with someone else's without telling them about it? That doesn't seem quite right."

"To hell with them," Nadine shot back. "I'm going to leave that hat right there. You go on out with them tonight and when you all get back, I'm going to show them, show them all, that a hat on the bed don't mean nothing at all."

Rick again shook his head, laid the outfit and a couple

of sixteenths down on the nightstand, and said, "Here, you won't have any trouble with these, will you? I think they want to go right away. We won't be gone long, maybe a couple of hours at the most. We're just going over to look at that hospital, the same one we looked at this morning."

The hospital was a large, sprawling brick building only one story high. It had inner gardens surrounded by wings of the building, which turned into yet more wings. Inside it was like one continuous corridor, broken up at intervals by little substations, which contained a waist-high counter enclosure, a switchboard, a few desks, and an aid station of sorts. There were always a couple of nurses hanging around these substations. They were the watchdogs, the ones Bob feared most, for if one of them spotted you, they would put out the alarm and then everybody would be on the alert and relay your movements until they ran you down. And for some reason, which Bob could never quite fathom, there were always a couple of policemen lounging around in any hospital of any size.

Bob's plan on this particular night was to have Diane and Rick each steal an automobile close to the hospital; drive them into the parking lot; and clip, smash, and back into as many cars belonging to doctors, nurses, and policemen as possible. This would provide a cover, distracting the attention of any police or hospital personnel in the general vicinity of the pharmacy.

So Diane and Rick each found a car, then followed one another into the hospital lot. Rick was the first to go into action as Diane parked and watched. There were two police cars pulled up beside the hospital entrance. Rick headed right between them at a hair-raising thirty-five miles an hour. Only three feet separated the two cars, so Rick got both of their rear fenders in the initial rush. Next he threw his car into reverse and floored the accelerator. His car clung to the smashed police cars for a second while his tires screamed and poured out smoke. Then, abruptly, the torn and intermeshed metal of the cars separated and away Rick roared again, until he came to a halt forty feet away against another late-model car.

The noise all this ramming around produced had everyone within hearing distance hanging out a window to watch the madman in the parking lot. And Rick kept right on working. He gave the police cars another shot for good measure, then he picked out an automobile behind and off to one side and gave it a bank shot that crumpled the right front fender. He was in the process of picking out another likely target when two cops came running out of the hospital less than a hundred yards away.

Then Diane got into the act. She held her horn down, causing one continuous blast, and squealed out of her position, toward the officers who were racing after Rick. She didn't hit either of them, but she didn't miss them by much either, and both went sprawling to the pavement. Diane kept going until she came to Rick, who had ditched his car and was now on foot. She stopped momentarily to let Rick in, then turned and took off burning rubber all the way out of the parking lot.

Bob heard the pandemonium from where he was hiding up against the building. "They'll probably talk about this one for years," he told himself, smiling.

Then Bob quickly smashed out a window and climbed into a vacant office. Once inside, he crossed the room,

stuck his head out the door into a long corridor, and not
seeing any nurses or anyone else, stepped across the
corridor to the locked entrance of the pharmacy. After
studying the door momentarily, he took a small pry bar,
slammed the tapered end into the crack between the
door and the jam at lock level, and snapped the other
end of the bar back. The door shot open with a noise
resembling a muffled shot.

Bob quickly entered and closed the door behind him.
It stayed in position, but with a piece of the jam gone, it
would open silently with the slightest pressure. That
wasn't good, so Bob pulled out a small piece of hard-
wood he had with him and wedged the door tight. Then
he went directly to the narcotics cabinets housed behind
a counter. The lockers were made of one-eighth-inch
sheet steel and were not all that imposing, except that
they could slow up a person with theft on his mind. Bob
looked over the locks. They were huge brass padlocks
and had not been in place during the day for him to
study. Damn, he thought, to get this far and then have to
back off, with the whole thing set up like it was.

He tried to wedge his pry bar between the horseshoe-
shaped bolt of the lock, but the bar was too big. Next he
tried to wedge it between the lock and the hasp, but the
bar slipped out.

"Fuck it," he said aloud. The sweat was pouring down
his face in rivulets, his clothes were getting damp, and his
hands were starting to shake. He tried to force his bar
into the crack beside the cabinet door, but the bar
jumped toward him every time he applied pressure. Next
he tried lifting the cabinet free from the wall, but it was
solid. He jammed the pry bar between the wall and the

cabinet and gave a mighty heave. The cabinet bent toward him, but it was obvious that this would take too long.

There was only one way left to attack the cabinet with the tools he had at his disposal. He stood back a ways and brought the wedge-shaped point of the bar down in a cutting motion, in an attempt to tear a hole in the sheet metal large enough to reach inside. He was in the process of doing this when a nurse heard the commotion and hurried to the pharmacy door. When it didn't open, she knew something illegal was happening inside. So she raced to the nearest nurses' station and sounded the alarm.

Immediately, hospital security forces, attendants, and maintenance men proceeded posthaste to the pharmacy wing. Bob got one cabinet open only to find it full of Demerol, better known to drug addicts as "dummy oil," and let out a loud "Ugh!" He was just beginning his attack on a second cabinet when the pharmacy door flew open behind the weight of two burly attendants. They came hurtling into the room, took one look at Bob, and immediately began to close in. He turned, swung his bar at them in a threatening manner, and leaped over to a window overlooking one of the quaint little gardens. With one swing of the bar, he smashed out the window and dove through it.

Bob landed on an outer sidewalk in a roll and when he scrambled to his feet, blood was streaming down his face. "Good God," he said to himself. "It's a damn good thing I'm in a hospital, because before I'm through, I may well need the assistance of one." Above him, an attendant was trying to climb out the broken pharmacy

window. Bob gave him a mild bop on the head with his
bar and headed for an exit door to another wing, leaving
the attendant struggling to get back in the room.

The exit door was locked. Assuming others would also
be locked, Bob smashed a gaping hole through the glass
top of the door, reached in to open it from the inside,
and headed down the corridor. At this point, Bob didn't
much care where he came out, as long as he came out
somewhere. He took a clean handkerchief out of his hip
pocket and tried to wipe the blood from his face. But it
was still flowing pretty good and it only smeared.

Bob noticed a rest room ahead, ducked in, and stared
at the damage in a mirror above the sink. Must have cut
an artery, he figured, watching the blood pump out of his
forehead in small but forceful streams. He washed his
face and head as best he could, held a compress of wet
paper towels to the wound, wiped up the sink and mirror,
and then retreated to a toilet booth. There he sat and
waited. Whenever someone entered, he would quietly
stand, step up on the toilet seat, and crouch there until
he was sure they had left. It wasn't until the third person
had come and gone that he realized this was the ladies'
room and not the men's. "Oh, well, so much the better,"
he muttered. "If I'm going to have to wrassle my way out
of this spot, I'd much rather do it with a bunch of women
than with a bunch of men."

By this time Diane and Rick had returned to their own
car and had driven to the place near the hospital where
they expected to rendezvous with Bob. There they sat,
fidgeting, and when a half hour elapsed with no sign of
Bob, they knew something had gone wrong.

"Bob's like a rabbit, in and out and no nonsense,"

Diane told Rick, "and that goes for a lot more than just a hospital pharmacy. This just ain't like him. He should have been here long before now, and he isn't, so something's not right. The damn joint must have an alarm, or someone must have spotted him coming out."

She couldn't imagine anyone stopping Bob when he was on his way out, though. He was like a damn tiger then. That was one time in his everyday existence when he wasn't an easygoing kind of guy. When circumstances rose up to threaten his life, liberty, and pursuit of happiness in returning from a score with an armload of narcotics, then and only then did the blood lust come out in him. Nothing could stop him. He would go to any lengths to get away. And that was why Diane was so worried. Finally she told Rick, "I'm going in there and see what happened. Maybe I can help him get away."

Rick shook his head. "No, Diane, don't do it. Bob said to wait for him here in the car and that's what we're going to do. You don't even know he's in trouble yet. He might not even have made his move. He might just be sitting up on a roof somewhere watching what-all has taken place and is now waiting for things to cool down before he tries to make his way over here to the car. No, you just stay here. If they've got him, we'll know soon enough. They couldn't have much of a jail in this town, so if we can't get him out on bond, we'll just break him out, you and me. We'll send Nadine on down the road, and we'll go up there with guns if we have to and just flat take him out."

"You'd do that?" Diane asked, slumping down in the seat. "Are you sure when it comes right down to it, that you could do that? What I mean is, that it's a lot goddamn easier to sit out here in the car tonight and talk

about it than it's going to be to go down to that jail
tomorrow night and do it. I hope you know that, Rick.''

"I know that, Diane. I know that, and I wouldn't have
committed myself if I hadn't thought it all out first. You
can depend on me.''

Neither Diane nor Rick said another word. They just
sat there worrying while the sun came up. They sat
through the early-morning hours and watched the milk-
man come and go, then various people leave for work. At
ten o'clock Diane finally admitted to Rick, "We might as
well give it up. He ain't coming. They got him, the bastards got him, I know it, I can feel it in my heart. The
bastards, the dirty bastards! If they've hurt him just one
little bit, I'll kill them, I'll kill them all!''

And then the sobs began. They came slowly at first and
then exploded into a thunderstorm as Rick started the
car and drove back to the motel.

There was an ominous silence as Rick and Diane entered their motel room. Rick called out, "Nadine," and
the only answering sound was the quiet hum of the heat-
ing system. He opened the bedroom door and noticed
that the hat was still on the bed, but Nadine was nowhere
to be seen. And then he saw her out of the corner of his
eye as he stepped over to the closet to see if her clothes
were still there. She lay crumpled beside the bed on the
floor. Her lips and face had a funny bluish hue to them.
An outfit hung out of the ditch in her arm. Blood had run
back into it, filling it up. It took a moment for Rick to
realize that she was not breathing, that she was indeed
dead.

"Oh, my God," Rick moaned, falling to his knees beside Nadine's cold, lifeless, stiffening body.

"I'm sorry, baby, I'm so sorry," he cried.

Rick knew he should never have gotten her into all this. Nadine was so sweet, so innocent, so lovely. Why couldn't he have just left her alone? Why had he wanted to change her? He had wanted to be understood. He had wanted a woman to look up to him, to learn from him, to love him. But he had not wanted her like this. Rick realized now, he had taken advantage of her innocence and had gotten her involved in something she didn't understand. And now she was gone forever.

"Oh, baby, I'm so sorry, so sorry. I'm sorry."

He cupped both his hands around her pale, lifeless hand.

"So cold."

He tried to lift her and hold her. The tears flowed freely as he rocked her in his arms. "Oh, baby, please, baby, oh goddamn, what can I do?"

And he completely broke down as Diane came striding into the room to see what was wrong. "Oh, my God," she said. "Not again!"

Diane was huddled over Rick with her arms around his neck, sobbing into his back when Bob came in the front door. His face, upper forehead, and one arm were covered with white medical tape and bandages. His coat was splotched with dried blood from hem to collar. "What in the hell is going on?" he asked, entering the bedroom.

Diane turned, took one look at his bedraggled appearance, and flew into his arms. "What did the bastards do to you? How did you ever get away? Did you get out on bond?"

The only thing that held Bob's eyes was the hat on the

bed. "Who put that hat on that goddamn bed?" he shouted.

Rick looked up at Bob. "She did, Bob," he choked. "She didn't really mean no one no harm by it, she was just going to prove to you all that it wouldn't affect us, that it was just a superstition, an old wives' tale, she called it. She just felt so bad about having run with that drawer that I went and let her have her own way, and look what happened. Oh God, it's all my fault. I shouldn't have let her do it. I should have stayed home with her. I shouldn't have left her alone."

Bob noticed for the first time what Rick was cradling in his arms. He had seen too many overdose cases not to know one when he saw one. "Who gave her the stuff? She couldn't have did that on no two sixteenths. What's she been doing, saving it up?"

And then he noticed the small bottle on the night-stand, next to the bent and blackened spoon Nadine had obviously used. He picked it up and held it up to the light. Only half of the contents remained in the bottle. "Where in hell did she get a hold of this?" he asked, thrusting the bottle out for Rick and Diane to see.

They didn't know. "What is it?" Rick asked.

"It's powdered Dilaudid. I knew there should have been another partially filled bottle in with that mess we got last night. I even said so at the time. She must have picked it up while we were collecting the bottles off the seat and floor, or she took it out of the sack while she stood by that house and waited for us. The stupid, con-niving bitch!"

Rick jumped up like he was slapped. "You can't call her

that! She's dead. Look at her," he sobbed. "She's dead!
Don't ever say anything bad about her!"

Bob shook his head in disgust. "She beat you, man.
Your own woman beat you out of part of your own cut on
a score. She got what she deserves. Not only that, the
dumb bitch threw a hex on us that we'll all be lucky to
survive. And not only that, she left us with an ODed stiff,
which is paramount to a murder beef in this state, if I'm
not mistaken. So if you want to do life over some dumb
broad that stole the stuff off you to kill herself with, go
ahead, be my guest. Only just forget you ever knew me,
you got that? You never heard of Diane and me. And for
chrissakes, get that goddamn hat off that bed, and get
that lousy stiff into the closet before the maid comes in to
change the beds. And you just better pray she don't find
it necessary to open that closet door, because that will
just about cinch us all up good if she does."

And with that, Bob backed out of the bedroom with
Diane still clinging to him and slammed the door.

"How did you ever get away?" Diane asked, looking up
at him. "We waited and waited all night. I was even going
to go in and try to find you or at least find out what
happened, but Rick, he didn't want me to go."

Bob stuck his nose down and nuzzled Diane's neck.
"It's all right, baby," he said. "Take it easy. I just stayed
in there too long. They ran in on me and I had to dive out
the window. I spent the rest of the night hiding out in a
women's rest room. I finally fell asleep, woke up about an
hour ago when some woman janitor came in to clean up
the place. She cleaned up all around me. I had to stall like
hell and keep on making just enough noise in there so it
was obvious the booth was occupied. Finally she went on

to do some work someplace else and I slipped out into the corridor. No sooner did I get out there than some nurse comes along, notices my condition, and asks me what happened. I make out like I'm a lot worse off than I am, stagger around a bit, and tell her that I'd come home drunk this morning and drove my car through the back of my garage and cut the hell out of myself, and that my wife put me in a cab and sent me to the hospital, and that when I got there and asked the directions to the emergency room, they told me where to go, but that somehow I got lost and that this was where I ended up. I don't know whether they actually bought my story or not, because they gave me some mighty funny looks, but they bandaged me up, sewed up a few cuts, and turned me loose. I don't think anyone followed me home, but they could have easily enough. I had to take a cab. I called here, but no one answered the phone."

"Oh, goddamn, hon, what are we going to do?" Diane said, shaking her head.

"Well, there isn't much point in trying to get Nadine out of here this morning, so get some stuff out, let's fix and think about it for a while. Jesus, I'm sick as a goddamn dog."

After Bob and Diane washed up a bit, fixed, and changed their clothes, they lay on their bed, thinking. "I know what," Diane exclaimed. "Let's pull her up into the attic and hide her that way for the day. At least then the maid won't be stumbling over her."

"You know what, Diane?" Bob said, pulling himself up on one elbow. "That's probably the best idea you've come up with in years. Come on."

They entered the bedroom, and found Nadine's body

where the hat had been. Rick was kneeling on the floor with his head down on the bed as though in prayer. Bob walked up to him, lifted him from behind, and dragged him out of the room.

"Diane, put about six of those sixteenths in a spoon. We got to get Rick here in bed. He's been up all night and probably don't know what the hell he's doing, do you, Rick? Okay, let's go now. You can lay down in our room."

So they hustled Rick into the other bedroom, fixed him up, laid him out on their bed, and turned their attention back to Nadine's corpse. Diane got up on a chair, opened the trapdoor, and climbed into the attic. Bob got the body over his shoulder in a fireman's lift and carried it to the closet. It took some doing to cram himself and the corpse into the closet, then struggle up on the chair and position Nadine so Diane could pull from above, but finally they managed to get the body into the attic, and just in time too. No sooner had they gotten down and put the trapdoor into place and moved the chair out of the closet than the doorbell rang. It was the maid. They let her in, explained that the man in the bedroom was sick, and hustled her through her chores until she was gone.

As the tension drained away, Bob sunk down in a chair and said, "Wow, what a fucking day, and it ain't over yet. Just how in the hell do I get in these situations anyway, Diane? Just answer me that. I mean, what the hell, I try to keep my business straight. I try to take care of my people. I even dole them out what I think they can use, just so this won't happen, and what happens? The dizzy broad steals some stuff off of me. Me, the guy that's carrying the whole goddamn outfit on my back like it was my own newborn son. You know what, Diane? I knew there should have been another bottle of that stuff, never just one full bottle. I even remarked about it. I kind of thought at the time that someone had swung with it, but I didn't think it was Nadine. Hell, I didn't think Nadine even cared about the stuff. I thought that probably Rick had got it and stashed it away for a rainy day. If I wasn't so softhearted I'd have shook down the whole crew, but who wants to accuse your friends of something like that? That's like stealing off your own family, and who the fuck would do that? Jesus, sweet Jesus, whatever I do any-more seems to somehow come out wrong. What the fuck ever happened to the good people, the real thieves, the guys and broads you could depend on?"

"I'll tell you what happened to them, they're all dead or in jail," Diane said. "I think we're a dying breed, baby. I think the day of the buffalo is gone forever. Pretty soon narcotics will be legal. They're already starting that with methadone, and when they're all legal, what'll you have? Nothing but easy riders and tramps. Ain't no good peo-ple no more because it isn't even mod to be a good person nowadays. It's whoever gets down first. Fuck your partner, fuck your partner's old lady, and steal every goddamn thing he's got, the first time he goes to jail on a roust and ain't home to protect his old lady and his stuff. These goddamn kids today, they ain't got no sense at all. They're all TV babies. They been watching people kill-ing and fucking each other on that goddamn boob tube since before they can remember, and that's all they know. Hell, they think it's legal, that it's the right thing to do."

"I know, hon. You can't change it, though. We just got

to grin and bear with it. Either that or clean up and live
the good life, and I don't think I could stand that. Come
on, let's go lay down for a while. The bedding's all
changed. Come on."

Diane followed Bob into the empty bedroom and together they stretched out on the bed. "Poor Nadine,"
Bob began, "just a goddamn kid. I really didn't much like
her. She just seemed too demanding, always wanting her
way, always wanting this, always wanting that. I guess if
I'd have had any premonition of how things were going
to come down for her, I'd have given in to her a little
more. Hell, I tried to be as nice as I could, but you can't
baby them any more than I do without spoiling them.
Hell, it's like trying to raise a couple of goddamn kids,
when you take on a couple like that and try to teach them
to steal. Do you know that, Diane? It's just like raising
children. All the hassles, all the petty jealousies, all the
what-ifs. I'm getting too old for this shit. I been stealing
dope and shooting dope all my life, and right now for the
very first time I wish maybe I had done something else. I
don't know what, because I don't know nothing else.
Maybe I should have taken up a trade in prison when
they were trying to teach everyone one; came out, picked
you up, got your kids back, and went that route. Jesus, I
can just see us now, fighting all goddamn day long and
drinking all night long to keep from fighting in the morning, yelling at the kids, screaming at each other, frustrated from dawn to dark every goddamn day because we
know there is a better way, because we've had it better.
Am I crazy, baby, or am I right? A lot of people hearing
me say all this would jump up and say I'm crazier than a
shithouse rat, and you know what, baby? I think maybe

they're crazy. Because at least I tried their way casually a couple of times and I didn't think it was shit. And there they sit. All they've done is maybe read a few bogus articles about dope fiends and the first conclusion that comes into their heads is that we're all no good, that we're all subhuman, that they're better than we are, that we ought to be locked up in a cage and kept there for the rest of our lives. And why? Because we want to do with our bodies what we ought to be entitled to do. They sit around and snivel about all the crime in the streets, and hell, all they got to do is make dope legal and cheap and they won't have any. And you know who's against that? The goddamn cops. They wouldn't be so big and important if they didn't have crime in the streets. They'd be bored to death without a dozen calls a night to keep them busy. Hell, the doctors want it legal, every god-damn one of them will tell you so. The pharmacists do too. Everybody does but the cops and a few politicians that are taking such a big rake off that they can't afford to have it legal. It's the goddamn prohibition thing all over again, and as long as organized crime can make a hundred billion dollars a year selling sugared-down heroin, and as long as the politicians and cops get their pay-offs, they'll never make it legal, if they can help it."

Diane snuggled up closer to Bob. "Relax, hon. You can't fight the whole world. Relax awhile. Things will work out. You remember what I said once about bad luck sometimes being good luck? Well, I think maybe that sometimes good luck can also turn around and come out bad. Look at that nice score you got right off the bat last night, and look at how it all turned out. Who can figure it all out? You can't, I can't, not if we sit and worry about it for a hundred years. All we can do is relax, try our best, hope like hell, and take things like they come—and laugh like hell when they come out wrong."

"You know, baby," Bob grinned, "I think that's maybe the most intelligent thing you ever come up with in your whole life. How about hopping up and getting some more stuff? I'll get the water and spoons. I sure do need something. That last jolt didn't seem to do much for me."

Ten minutes later the phone rang. Bob looked at it suspiciously for a few moments, then gingerly picked it up.

"Is this Mr. or Mrs. Hughes?"

"Mister," Bob said.

"Are you planning on checking out today?"

"No, why?"

"Well, I'm sorry, sir, but when you registered, we asked you how long you intended to stay and you said only a couple days. We had prior commitments in the form of reservations for this room, and had we known you were going to stay so long, we would have informed you upon your arrival that we would have to have your room today."

"You mean I got to move out right now?"

"Yes, sir," the woman answered. "It would be most convenient if you would do so."

"Well, you just listen here. One of our guests is very ill and I just don't feel that we want to up and try to move to another motel right now, today. How about in the morning? We'll leave first thing in the morning."

"I'm sorry, sir, but I will have to ask you to leave now. You see, we are having a sheriffs' convention here in town and all these rooms have been reserved for them, as long as ninety days ago. We just couldn't refuse them their rooms after having made such a commitment."

"Wait a minute. Wait. Let me come down to the office and talk to you. I'll be right down."

"What was that all about?" asked Diane when Bob hung up.

"They want to chase us out of our room."

"Now?"

"Yep, right now. Seems they're having a sheriffs' convention here and they need the room."

"They're what?"

"You heard me. I'm going to see the manager and see if I can't get them to let us keep this room another day, and if I can't, be ready for anything, because we're going to have to do something. Jesus Christ, a sheriffs' convention, no less. Why couldn't it be a pharmacists' convention, or better yet, an undertakers'?"

Bob walked into the motel office and confronted a large, stately, smiling blonde behind the counter. "I'm sorry, Mr. Hughes," she said. "You should have let us know you intended to stay this long. We'd have warned you of our commitments."

"Listen, lady. I got a partner in that motel room that's got the mumps. I'm scared to move him. What if they should go down on him? Hell, we'd hit you with a lawsuit that would ruin you. Now, can't you juggle those rooms around a bit or get the intendeds a reservation somewhere else?"

"I'm sorry, Mr. Hughes. I do wish we could accommodate you and your party, but I'm afraid it's out of the question."

"Well, just you let me tell you something then, lady. I'm going to telephone the health board right now and ask them what they think about this matter. They may just quarantine our room. They're not going to let some poor dude walk in and get exposed to the mumps while staying in your motel, I know that, and all I want is one more day. I don't want to get stuck here either, and the doctor says that in one more day he can travel. So how about it, huh?"

"Well, if that's the case, you go on back to your room. I'll have to talk to the manager. Perhaps we can reserve them a room somewhere else just for this one night."

When Bob walked out of the motel office, he could feel the perspiration running down his chest and stomach.

"Well?" Diane asked when he returned.

"I think they're going to let us keep it one more night."

Diane sighed. "Good God, how are we ever going to get her out of here if the whole place is full of drunken cops coming and going all night?"

"I don't know, Diane, I really don't know."

"Maybe we could just head on out and leave her up there."

Bob looked astounded. "Diane, are you mad? She'd be oozing down out of the attic in less than a week. These people around here have seen her. They're going to remember that she was with us. No, we got to get her out tonight."

Bob sat for a long time thinking. Finally he snapped his fingers and said, "Okay, here's what we do. You run on downtown, go to a luggage shop and buy one of those plastic zip-in suit hangers. We'll get her in that and I'll haul her out over my back, like it's full of suits, topcoats, and such. Get a colored one. Don't get one of those see-through outfits. And buy a shovel too."

Before Diane left, however, she and Bob sat around fixing, time after time. Diane tried to start a conversation once or twice, but Bob ignored her. He sat in a big chair and just stared at the floor when he wasn't engrossed in whatever he was fixing. Finally Diane asked, "Her death really got to you, didn't it, Bob?"

Bob considered the question for a while, then looked straight at her for the first time that afternoon. "Yeah, I suppose you could say that. I'm not exactly thrilled over her having left us in such an abrupt manner. Yes, I suppose you could say that I am slightly upset. Aren't you?"

"I don't mean that, Bob. I've seen you around other overdose cases and you never got like this."

"Like what?"

"Oh, I don't know. Just different."

"Oh yeah, well, I'll tell you what's wrong. I'm scared. I'm scared to fucking death that some big fucking cop is going to come rumbling through that door any minute and say, 'Out, this is my fucking room, out.'"

"Oh, come on, Bob. You've been in tighter positions than this before."

"No, Diane, I don't think I ever have," Bob answered, slowly shaking his head.

"What about the time they killed your partner, Danny, when you was coming out of that drugstore over on Eleventh?"

"Diane, I was running, doing something. I didn't have time to get like this. I wasn't just sitting and waiting and thinking and sweating."

Diane changed the subject. "Did they ask you about all your bandages while you were over in the motel office?"

"No, they didn't say a word. I kind of wondered about that. Maybe they were so worried about their prior commitments, they forgot to ask."

Eventually, Diane left to get the suit carrier and shovel. When she returned, Bob was where she had left him, sitting on one end of the couch hovered over a coffee table fixing up different solutions. After watching for a while, Diane observed, "You're going to keep that up, Bob, then me and Rick will have to stash you up in the attic too."

Bob stared at Diane for a while. Finally he grinned and put down what he was fixing. "Yeah, I suppose you're right," he said. "The damn stuff never seems to help much when you really need it, anyhow. I wonder why that is? When you're really depending on something, it never seems to come out quite the way you expect it to. Have you ever noticed that, Diane?"

"Bob, go in and lay down for a while."

Bob grinned sheepishly, got up slowly from the couch, and headed for the bedroom. "Jesus, Diane, does everyone have the ups and downs we do, or is it just because we're dope fiends that things always seem so topsy-turvy?"

"Bob, go lay down awhile and quit thinking all that crap. Nothing you can do now is going to change anything that's already done. You can't bring her back, Bob, even as smart and determined as you are, you can't bring her back. She's gone. She's gone forever."

But Bob hadn't quite made it to the bed when the phone rang. He strode over and answered it.

"Mr. Hughes?"

"Yes."

"I'm sorry it took me so long to answer your request for an added day, but the manager wasn't here then and I just got to talk to him. He said okay, but Mr. Hughes, you will have to be out of that room tomorrow. We have to have it."

"Well, thank you, miss. We'll get out in the morning. We're all packed now and raring to go. The doctor says one more night's rest should take our guest out of the danger area, and I want to thank you. We really appreciate all you've done for us."

Bob hung up the phone and turned to Diane. "We got the room. Christ, it must be four o'clock, huh? I wonder what time will be best for what we have in mind. Can't be too late. I don't want to be driving around with a stiff in my car in the wee hours. We'll just have to wait and see. Maybe we can get her in the car while it's late and then wait until morning to take her out in the country somewhere."

"You'd better get an alarm clock at the office so we'll be able to wake up when we want to, Bob, because once we fall asleep there's no telling when we'll wake up again."

"That's a good idea, Diane. You go get it, will you? I hate to go outside with all these bandages on me. I look too conspicuous."

"Oh Jesus, I should have kept my mouth shut. Okay, I'll get it."

So they got the alarm clock and then both lay on the bed. Within minutes Diane was snoring lightly. Bob just watched the ceiling as though he expected Nadine to come crashing through it at any moment. Finally he rose and went back to the living room. He fixed up some Dilaudid and then lay back on the couch and tried to relax. Nothing seemed to help, so he gave up and just sat staring at the floor. He was still there examining the patterns in the carpet when the alarm went off at four in the morning. After the third ring, Diane reached over and snapped it off. Then she got up and stumbled into the living room.

"Are you still up?"

"No, I slept for quite a while," Bob lied. "I just got up a while ago and came in here to fix."

"Well, I suppose we had better go up and get her down out of there," said Diane. She yawned and threw back her head to get the hair out of her face. "Jesus, I wonder how much noise it's going to make."

This time it was Bob who crawled into the attic. It was all he could do to touch the body. He'd been thinking about her too much and now the whole thing was blown out of proportion. Finally he crouched on his knees and grabbed Nadine under her arms and tried to stuff her down the hole, but her stiffened limbs didn't easily yield to his efforts. By the time he had lowered the corpse at arm's length through the opening, he was ready to vomit.

Diane stood on the chair and tried to ease Nadine down on her back. But the weight was too much. Diane's legs buckled and down she went in an entangled heap with the chair and the body.

Drained of energy and spirit, Bob just lay in the attic looking down at the mess. Meanwhile a neighbor, no doubt some sheriff, pounded on the walls and shouted, "For chrissakes, keep the noise down over there!"

Diane finally worked her way out from under the heap, dragged Nadine's body to a bedroom, and sat it up in a chair as Bob climbed down. It took them almost a half hour to get the corpse stuffed into the suit carrier to the point that it could be zipped closed.

"Good God, what a hassle," Bob said, mopping the sweat off his brow when they finished the gruesome task. "We should have gotten Rick up to help us. Perhaps then he'd supervise his old lady's habits better and we wouldn't have these messes all the time."

"You know better than that, Bob," Diane disagreed. "It wasn't his fault, no more than it was yours. It was just one of those things. They happen. No one can reason just how or why, but they do. Now, do you think you're going to be able to carry her out in this thing? That girl is heavy as hell. I never thought of her as weighing as much as she does. Christ, she'd have been fat in another couple of years."

Bob went to the window and looked out into the parking lot. All he could see was cop cars. It looked like his car and pickup were the only vehicles in the lot that didn't have radio antennas and red lights sticking out all over them.

"Good Christ, Diane, look at that damn parking lot! I never seen nothing like it. I don't know if I got nerve enough to cross to the car with her on my back. Look at that fucking parking lot!"

Diane stepped beside him and looked outside. She drew in her breath sharply, then sighed and said, "You can do it, Bob. You got to do it. I can't. She's too heavy. I don't want to trust Rick with it and neither do you. You got to do it."

Bob stretched nervously and flung back the drapes. "Okay," he said. "You go out first, unlock the car, we'll use that. Look around a bit while you're doing it. See if anyone is lurking about. Check out the office too."

Diane put on her coat and reached up to kiss Bob. "Don't worry so, Bob," she said. "We'll make it, we always do, don't we?" And then she smiled, turned to the door, and headed for the parking lot.

Bob stood around and fidgeted. He wanted to watch Diane from the draped window, but he knew it would be a mistake to do so.

Diane was gone for about ten minutes. "We're all set," she said when she returned. "The car door's open and I didn't see anyone at all. The office is dark and all the rooms have the windows draped."

"Good," said Bob, picking up the bundle from the floor. "Now, you open the door, Diane, and go out ahead of me. Keep your eyes open and keep looking around. If anyone spots us, get under that wheel and get the engine started and get us the fuck out of here before they can come over and look us over very good, you got that?"

Diane nodded and opened the motel door. It was fifty feet to the car and Bob was huffing and puffing as though he'd just run a mile by the time they got there. Getting the suit carrier into the back seat was no easy task, but Bob supposed it would have been a lot harder without the carrier.

After they had locked the car and returned to the motel room, Diane noticed Bob's clothes were soaked. "Wow, what a drag," he said, reaching up idly and wiping his dripping forehead. "I mean, that broad was heavy. You're right, Diane, she would have been fat in a couple of years. Jesus, I'm glad she decided to go and do her thing now instead of waiting until then. I'd have never made it."

Bob looked at Diane and tried to grin, but it didn't quite come out right. He almost seemed to be a little kid about to bawl. And the perspiration continued to seep out of him at an alarming rate. Soon his feet were squishing around in his shoes. He felt terrible, he felt as if he needed another fix, and that's all he'd been doing all night, pumping it in.

"I'm going to take a shower, Diane," he finally said. "How about going up in the attic and getting our stuff down and dividing it up. We'll give Rick the car and the stuff we sent ahead to those bus depots. Figure it all out. Don't count him short. Give him the big end."

Diane stared at Bob until he turned his eyes away. "What are you thinking about doing, Bob? What've you got on your mind?"

Bob let his eyes slide around the room evasively. He started to speak a couple of times, then said nothing. He turned and went through the bedroom to the shower.

When Diane heard the water running, she sighed and got out of her chair. Then she climbed up into the attic and got the stash.

Bob stayed in the shower a long time. When he came out, Rick was up and fixing and Diane sat in the middle of the floor with three piles of narcotics bottles around her. No one said anything until Rick finished. He cleaned his outfit, put it away, and asked Bob, "What's happening?"

Rick seemed all right. He seemed to have gotten himself back together. He looked ready for anything. Bob watched him in quiet amazement, wishing he could be like that, or at least appear that way. He couldn't, though. He showed how he felt and he knew it, and that made it all the worse. He sat there and let the question go past him, leading Rick to wonder if he had heard it, or understood it, or if maybe the question was just too ridiculous to answer. Finally Rick coughed and asked again, "What's going on? We going to split up or something? Hell, I didn't know nothing about that stuff she had. I had no idea she had that stuff or that she would pull anything like that."

Both Rick and Diane waited for Bob to say something. Bob evaded their eyes and studied everything in the room slowly, as though this were the first time he had been there. Finally his eyes returned to them and he said, "That ain't got nothing to do with it, Rick. I mean, I don't blame you for what happened. It's like Diane says, it just happened and there isn't nothing we can do about it now but get rid of the evidence. The thing is that I've been thinking about heading on back to the coast. I think maybe I'll go on down and get on that twenty-one-day methadone withdrawal program, get my head together a bit, look at this old world with clearer vision, so to speak, and try to figure some things out."

"You're kidding!" Diane exclaimed.

"No, I'm not, Diane," Bob said, slowly shaking his head.

"Well, I'm not going on no withdrawal program, so what's going to happen to me?"

"Do whatever you want, Diane. Take whatever you need or whatever we got. I only need enough to get me to the coast, a little stuff and a little money. You can have the rest of it. You and Rick can split it up any way you like.''

"You mean this is it, that you're leaving me?" Diane asked coldly.

"No, I'm not leaving you. You asked, what about you, what you were going to do, and I told you what I'd do for you. That's all I can do. I haven't got anything else. If you want to come along with me, fine.''

"No, thanks, buster! Not a fucking word do you mention to me about all this! Right out of a clear blue sky you're going to clean up your hand and you know I can't, so this is just a way to get rid of me, right? Well, I'll tell you one thing right now, Bob. You didn't have to go to all this trouble to get rid of me. All you had to do was say, 'Get out,' and I'd have gone. You don't have to come up with all this bullshit!''

Rick just stood around looking embarrassed as Bob continued to act evasive and unsure of himself. His movements were jerky and a twitch began in his right cheek. He coughed as if in need of something to do and finally said, "We better get the rest of our stuff in the car and get the hell out of here. You follow us in the pickup, Rick. When we come back to town, I'll take the truck and turn it in on my way to the Greyhound station.''

After driving up and down gravel roads for most of the morning, Bob picked his spot. It was a heavily wooded area away from farms and logging operations.

"Get the shovel, Diane," Bob said after they had pulled to the shoulder of the rutted gravel road. "I'll handle her," he said, nodding to the corpse. "You, Rick, stay here and see that nobody comes along and wants to know if we're having a picnic or something."

Bob seems to have perked up some, Rick noticed. Just give him a job to do and he can help himself, no matter how down he might be otherwise.

Rick sat slumped in the front seat of the car and watched Bob drag the suit carrier with Nadine's body in it out of the car and off into the brush. Rick wondered how she had done it, whether she had meant to, or if she had just accidentally put too much in the spoon. She really hadn't seemed all that depressed. She didn't like the way things were going, but that in itself didn't seem excuse enough for such a drastic move. She must have just been ignorant and used too much, Rick decided. Powdered Dilaudid was pretty deadly stuff to fool around with, especially if you didn't know what you were doing.

Now it seemed that Bob blamed him for it, and by rights, he probably was to blame, at least more than anybody else. A dope fiend or thief was supposed to take care of his old lady, watch out for her, see that she didn't get hurt, that she didn't speak at the wrong moment or snitch or ever threaten to. It was funny, the relationship between a doper and his old lady. Old ladies were considered a luxury among dopers who could afford them, for what could they do for you besides offer a little companionship? If they didn't keep their mouths shut and their business straight, nothing! And if they ran their heads a lot, like most of them do, they were a bitch.

Rick's thoughts turned again to Bob. Jesus, the guy sure was acting funny. Looks as though he's really going to throw up his hands and go out on his own. Something sure was going on in his head.

Rick remembered the first time he had met Bob and
Diane. He had just gotten out of the joint in California,
and had headed north because he'd heard it was better
up there and also because he just didn't think he could
stand another jolt in those California prisons.

When he had gotten off the bus in the city, he'd
checked into a fleabag hotel and then just wandered the
streets looking for someone he might know. It took him a
week to do just that. And the guy he found was no prize
either, and besides that, he didn't even know the guy
very well. He had just seen him around the prison yard.
They got to talking anyway, and it seemed that this guy
didn't have any more going for him than Rick, and he'd
been out for six months.

He partnered up with his acquaintance and began
shoplifting, and that's how he met Bob and Diane. His
friend had taken him over to Bob's to try to make a trade,
some clothes for some narcotics. Bob was arrogant as
hell and Rick hated him at first. Bob seemed to come on
so strong and so shitty. He acted like everyone else in the
world was below him and had to do what Bob wanted or
they weren't any good. This went on for some time until
one day Bob asked Rick to stay behind when he and
Tommy had come by for a trade. Bob was just as abrupt
as ever, but when the door closed on Tommy's heels,
Bob turned with a complete change of mood and asked,
"Say, Rick, you want to go to work for me and get your
ass off the streets for a while?"

Bob had somehow turned that little phrase into a chal-
lenge with a little respect for Rick as a person thrown in,
as if he were actually saying, "You're a good man and I
know you'll work out. All you need is a little help and

advice and we can make a great team and take on the
whole goddamn world."

Rick said yes, but with misgivings. He could hardly say
he liked Bob at this point and he wasn't sure he could do
what Bob would no doubt ask of him. He soon found out
that Bob's act was all a sham, that he acted nasty to
outsiders because he was so good to those he associated
with, and that he just couldn't stand to have too many
friends. It wasn't long before Rick realized that he'd
been hearing about Bob all his life, even way down in
Southern California. They talked about the heeler who'd
try anything, about the guy who had raided more drugstores on the West Coast than anyone else, the dude who,
even when he held big stuff, still wouldn't sell narcotics
to anyone.

Then Rick got to thinking about how he had met Nadine. He had entered a small drugstore at closing time
with Bob and Diane, and there was no one in the store
but the girl at the cash register in the main part of the
store and the druggist in the back. Rick was supposed to
engage the girl in conversation, distracting her until Bob
and Diane were ready to make their move. And the
strangest thing happened. Rick and that sexy blond girl
hit it off not more than ten seconds into their conversation. The blood rushed to Rick's head as he decided right
there on the spot that before him was the nicest, cutest,
cuddliest young thing he had ever laid eyes on. And he
could tell she was getting just as excited as he was, the
way she moved forward ever so slightly with the warmth
literally leaping out of her bosom, the way she smiled,
pleased with the size and strength and looks of the man
before her.

By the time it was Rick's duty to put a hammerlock on her, while Diane held a gun on the pharmacist and Bob dived for the drawers, Rick felt peculiar touching, moving against this sweet girl, but in such a grossly crude manner, as she looked up at him weakly, more puzzled than scared, almost embarrassing him, not for being a brute but for not trusting her. And finally Rick could stand it no longer and he hollered over to Bob, "Bob, she's coming with me." Bob had looked up, his hands full of bottles, with the most incredulous look on his face, and said, "What?" Rick had gone on, "You heard me, Bob, I want this woman. You got a woman, why can't I have one?" And Bob had stood there with a pained and bewildered look on his face, almost forgetting what he was doing, and Diane had started laughing so hard that she nearly dropped the gun and fell to the floor in a fit. But Nadine, she just looked up at Rick, and rather than being surprised or outraged by his presumption, told him with her soft eyes, That's more like it, you're my man.

And now she was dead. Nadine was gone. Would there ever be another like her, Rick wondered.

Bob was digging well out of sight of the road. The sod and roots almost beat him at first, but he kept chopping and hacking and digging and chopping until he finally had a shallow grave about two feet deep. Then he dragged the plastic carrier with Nadine's body in it to the hole and slid it in. At the last moment, he unzipped the end of the carrier and looked down. Nadine lay there with a surprised look on her face and her eyes open, staring back. Bob shuddered, zipped the case shut, and began to fill in the hole. When he was through, he absently stumbled around the area picking up random sticks and breaking off parts of bushes to use in covering the newly disturbed earth. Diane finally put an end to this by demanding, "Let's go, Bob. That's enough."

Bob then turned, almost as if he had no will of his own left and had been awaiting the command to send him back to the car.

Once there, he got his suitcases and clothes out of the car, put them in the rear of the pickup, and without another word or even so much as a glance at his friends, got behind the wheel, started the engine, turned in the seat to see out the rear window, and began backing out along the narrow country road.

Diane watched from the weeds beside the road. She watched him disappear from sight and kept standing there as if waiting for him to change his mind at the last minute and return. Fifteen minutes passed and finally Rick stirred in the front seat of the car and stuck his head out the window. "What's happening? Why all the fuss?" he asked her.

Diane shrugged her shoulders and dropped her eyes. "Hell, I don't know."

"Do you think he's really going to do all that stuff, withdraw and everything?"

Diane's body seemed to sag from the weight of her head and shoulders as she slowly made her way to the passenger's side of the car. "Yeah, I suppose he is," she said. "If there's one thing I've never heard, it was Bob tell me he was going to do something that he didn't at least try."

"Shit, how long do you think he'll last? A week, a month, a few days?"

"You got a lot to learn yet, buster," Diane said, looking directly at Rick as she climbed in the car. "But if you're careful, got the guts, and really want to become a thief, just maybe I'll be able to teach you how. Quit worrying about Bob. He'll do his own thing and whichever way it turns out, it will be right for him. You just start worrying about us. Now, I know you're ten years younger than I am, but I'm not looking for romance anyway. I'm looking for someone with guts. You had it easy with Bob, too easy, in fact. You'd have never learned nothing with him, really. Oh, you'd have saw how it was done, all right, but that ain't nothing like having to go in and lead the charge yourself. So if you think you can handle all that, we'll team up here and now. You get you an old lady and I'll get me an old man, and we won't pick them because they're beautiful people, we'll pick the ones that will make the best thieves in our heeling crew, and, baby, everyone will dive on this crew. It won't be no one-man show. Whoever gets lined up first will do the thing, and no slipping and sliding either, or down the road they go. We'll drive them crazy. We'll give those druggists a show that will keep them entertained for weeks while they sit around telling their friends about it. Hell, they probably won't even mind losing their little bit of stuff. You just stick with me, Rick, and I'll show you what it's all about. Bob was too soft anyway. He couldn't hurt a flea, you know, and couldn't fight a lick. Damn near every pharmacist on the coast has beaten him up at one time or another. Jesus, he sure could take a whipping, though."

And Diane smiled, thinking about all the crazy crap her

Bob had done through the years, as Rick wheeled the car off the gravel road onto the highway and headed toward the next rendezvous point. Yeah, she thought, the sonofabitch was all heart and brains without anything to back it up. Once they'd even killed his partner in a pharmacy robbery because Bob just couldn't shoot back. He didn't run out either, he finally just threw down his gun and tried to drag his partner out of there. It was a wonder they hadn't killed him as well. Diane shrugged to herself. "Oh well, they say that God looks out for drunks and fools, and He's sure enough looked out for Bob on occasion, and maybe he'll look out for him now too." It was going to be rough, though, what with the law all uptight about that shooting he'd set up and all. And that thing wasn't really like Bob either. Well, maybe he was changing in his autumn years, Diane figured. He sure did switch over mighty fast. She still could hardly believe it. Jesus, there had to be more to it than that, not just some broad ODing. Bob was soft as putty all right, but he'd been through all that crap before, the cleaning up and the burying of bodies. It was such a common occurrence among dope fiends that just about everyone who was involved in the drug trade had run through the course at least a couple of times. And the worst part of it all, thought Diane, was that she really did love Bob. She always had and probably always would. He was so good to her in so many ways. She had been with others, but none of them had made her as happy as Bob. Even if they could steal more and larger bags of dope and became really accomplished and really began bringing in the loot, they didn't seem to last long. They were too impatient and couldn't pace themselves like Bob. Either that or they just got so ringy eventually from all the dope they stole that they began to get visions of grandeur and did something exceedingly stupid and either got themselves busted or killed. Now, this Rick, he was a slick one. He never bitched a bit about staying in the background. She'd have to prime him up a bit and maybe push to get him in motion. But maybe that was good. At least he wasn't impatient and he did seem to have a little sense. And those two were very good and unusual traits among the thieves who made up the drug circuit. Now, just maybe, if she worked everything out well in advance and could control the goofy bastard, just maybe they could work up a good crew.

And as Rick tunelessly whistled and leisurely drove north along the highway, Diane ran through all her drug-stealing schemes. She thought of who they might try to recruit as soldiers in their crew, and where they would begin their operations should they get far enough along with her plans to begin working out again.

And while she was plotting, Bob was checking in the rented pickup after dropping off his luggage at the Greyhound station, and then slowly walking back to buy himself a ticket for the next bus to the coast.

When Bob took his seat near the back of the bus, he immediately adjusted it back as far as it would slide and tried to relax. But he couldn't bring his body to do it. He squirmed and moved his legs and arms around, trying to find a comfortable position, but without success. He brought the seat forward and tried sitting straight up. Then he tried various seat positions between the two extremes. Nothing worked.

Next he attempted to find something of interest in the

scenery along the highway, watching the rolling hills, the
rocks and streams slide by his window. They didn't mean
anything to him. He couldn't relate to the wilds. He had
never known any outdoor places unless it was some
briar-covered hill obstructing the way to some small
town where he planned to rip off the pharmacy.

Bob smiled as he thought of all the wooded areas he
had crossed and never seen, that he had just blundered
his way through, coming and going. He remembered
one particular night when he and Johnny Palmer had
fought three miles of tangled brush in a driving rain-
storm just to get to a drugstore without being seen. The
town's cop always sat all night at the lone signal light on
the one main street. It was virtually impossible to drive in
and out of that town without him spotting you. So they
had taken to the brush.

It was about an hour per mile, thrashing through that
dark, wet brush. And then when they finally reached the
pharmacy, the side door that Bob was so sure he could
spring open proved to have a chain and padlock looped
through the door's inside handles. It had almost beaten
them, but Bob was not ready to quit quite yet, until some
cars happened by and they had to back off and head for
the brush.

Bob was physically beat. He sat on the soggy, cold
ground with the wind whipping rain against his face,
trying to think of some implement they could fashion out
there in the wilds or steal from some garage. They had a
crowbar with them, but a chain is virtually impossible to
force with a crowbar. And then a long freight train came
chugging toward town, and Bob knew he had that drugstore beaten. He jumped off the wet grass and told

Johnny, "This is it, partner. That sweet old train is not only going to cover any noise we might have to make, it's going to completely cut off any chance of traffic passing through from the other side of town."

So Johnny put his fingers in the partially opened double door to force the crack as wide as it would go. Then Bob brought the heavy end of the crowbar down on the chain. It took many clanging blows and every time Bob hit the chain, the force of the blow would violently slam the doors on the bar and Johnny's fingers. But the bar stopped the doors just enough so that instead of broken and crushed fingers, all Johnny got were bruised ones.

Then they both dashed in behind the counters and began shaking down the place. Bob quickly found the narcotics stash in a large metal locker. It opened easily with the crowbar's leverage. They scooped up what they wanted and headed back into the brush, which again fought them step for step as if they were up against stubborn antagonists who would only yield to someone even more stubborn and desperate. And when they finally returned to the car where Diane had waited all night, she immediately asked, "Did you get any blues?"

Bob smiled to himself. He wondered if Diane would ever change. He doubted it. Diane was Diane, one of a kind, the only one made out of that particular mold before it was intentionally broken and cast away. Diane could love a man as much as any woman. The only thing is, Bob thought, she loved her man for different reasons and in a different light. Like other women, she loved a man who could produce, and she loved with great intensity. But if he didn't produce where she wanted him to produce, well then, that was it, good-bye to her man. She might think she loved the man himself, but it was the narcotics bag she'd follow, given a choice. Dope was her whole life, and without narcotics to steal and pharmacies to beat, Diane would no doubt dry up and wither away, Bob figured. She'd been out on the front lines for so long fighting the battles in the never-ending war that she didn't know anything else, nor did she dream of any exotic, romantic situation. Nothing could replace the lifestyle she led. Her children could be dragged off to an orphanage or driven out hungry into the streets and Diane would keep right on doing her thing. Oh, she might stop a minute and sympathize with them. She might even help them if she were in a position to do so. But Diane loved Diane just a little too much to ever think of giving up the ultimate, which to her was being with a crew heeling pharmacies. The day-to-day excitement with her man, the freewheeling, the narcotics—that was all Diane wanted out of life, that and nothing more.

Bob knew he had lost Diane, as much as she professed to love him, as much as she actually thought she did. She would never give up her present way of life. And why should she? Then she'd literally be nothing, just another frustrated housewife facing a daily life of boredom and drudgery. Now she was a queen, an expert in her field. Others sought her advice, and not just women, men as well. Lots of women had tried to copy her lifestyle, but few had the nerve, the heart, and the stamina to succeed. Diane had forsaken all the security-seeking the average housewife is preoccupied with. She didn't particularly care what her man looked like, how he acted, or what he said to her during breakfast. She could put up with any-

thing as long as he was a successful drug thief, as long as
she could be queen of a select group. Diane was getting
on in years, and they hadn't been easy ones, but it didn't
really matter all that much. In her world, as long as she
kept her fire and kept her old man out hustling, she'd be
the someone she had never been in her youth.

Bob smiled to himself as he remembered the first time
he'd seen Diane. He had just been released from the
state penitentiary. He was young, impatient, and eager to
get back into the action. But first he needed an automobile to get to and from the pharmacy he had in mind. He
had scoured the city looking for someone who would
either lend him one or go along and drive while he
ripped off the joint. Instead he found Diane. She was
baby-sitting for some friends of his, and while waiting for
the friends to return, he began talking to her.

She was young, very young and no doubt quite impressionable. She was also cute and very much the little lady
of the world. Healthy, good-looking, and just released,
Bob impressed her no end. The first thing she knew, she
was telling him all about her school activities, her likes
and dislikes, and her numerous minor romances.

Bob sat and grinned at her. He liked what he saw, and
the next thing he knew, he was telling her all about
himself. When he mentioned the part about just being
released from prison, he noticed her flinch, and he
thought to himself, now she's no doubt wondering just
what she's doing trapped all alone in this house with a
ringy convict. However, her smile soon returned and
Bob felt that everything was going to be all right.

Diane had fixed ideas about such things as convicts,
but somehow, Bob just didn't fit the image. He was actu-

ally shy, he was personable, and he seemed very inter-
ested in her. He wasn't the aggressive type and Diane
began to suspect that here was a man who would not only
love and respect her, but one she could manipulate any
way she chose. She later found out that some of her first
impressions were true, but that no matter what she said
or did or threatened to do, no matter how much she
begged or pleaded, she could not deter Bob from his
pharmacies. And when she finally began to realize this,
she gave up trying to straighten him out and joined him
in his illegal activities. At first she did it out of spite. She
wanted to show him just how ridiculous the whole thing
was. But it wasn't long before she became completely
submerged in the world of narcotics. And now one might
say that Diane had passed Bob. Bob got to thinking
about that, about how his woman was about to go him
one better, and he started smiling to himself, and the
smiles built until he couldn't help himself. He let a few
chuckles slip out, then laughed outright, until stares
from fellow passengers cut him short.

Bob eased back into his seat and began reliving his first
trip cross-roading with Diane. He had come to her house
the day after their first meeting for the sole purpose of
conning her out of her car. And he ended up spinning a
long yarn about all the money that they could easily pick
up by cross-roading through Canada and southeastern
Alaska. She fell for his story all the way, but instead of
just letting him take the car and travel on, she demanded
to be allowed to come along. At first Bob didn't know
what to think, whether she just wanted to be near him or
if she was really that concerned over the fate of her ten-
year-old automobile. He wasn't exactly an authority on

females, having spent more than ten of his tender twenty-five years in various penal institutions. He only knew what he had picked up in prison yards, where there is always an oversupply of men who know all there is to know about women. And what Bob had heard about these women seemed to in no way relate to the cute little girl he knew as Diane. He was beginning to like and respect her and he thought she'd no doubt be real good people if she'd just get off that kick of always trying to deter him from his illegal activities.

So they left for Alaska in Diane's old beat-up Dodge, without having so much as kissed, let alone slept together. Bob didn't know what to do to encourage such a situation and Diane didn't quite know what to expect. Bob seemed to want more of a road partner than a girlfriend or wife. Diane had been around a little. She knew what love and sex was all about, or so she thought until she finally did somehow fall into bed with Bob. Bob wasn't using narcotics at the time, primarily because he didn't have any outfits. But he did have some speed and he was using that. It was better than nothing and besides, he had a lot of driving to do. Back in those days, Bob did the driving, unless it was a getaway situation.

And so, when time and a motel room finally caught up with them, Bob, full of speed, launched himself at her and she accepted him because she supposed it was expected of her and that it was a part of her newly found profession. Until then, Diane really hadn't had much good to say about sex. It was just a messy, painful scourge heaped upon her, along with a lot of other garbage. But with Bob, sex was different. He was not only tender and considerate, he was an inexhaustible lover as

well. He went on for hours at a time, trying his best to
make up for all the time he had lost. He really didn't
know exactly what he was doing. He was making all his
moves on pure instinct, and obviously some of them
were the right ones. And once Bob became confident of
his style, with the aid of that speed to drive him on, he
conquered Diane then and forever.

Bob wasn't like the other males Diane had experi-
mented with, who came on with the rushed, panting,
lust-filled technique that seemed to please them but left
her feeling dirty and misused. Bob had a speed-driven,
unquenchable thirst for sex. Diane took it for love and
gave back as much as she was presented with. And so
they got caught up in a sexual wrestling match that went
on for weeks. Finally the veins in Diane's upper legs
ruptured from the constant straining, the arching of her
back and the thrusting of her hips. At first she didn't
know what was wrong. Her legs hurt and she couldn't
walk. Finally, with much concern, Bob took her to a doctor and then to a hospital. The doctors there never did
quite figure out what had caused her ailment and neither
did Diane or Bob until years later when it happened
again. So when Bob eventually got her out of the hospital
up in Prince George, British Columbia, and took her
home to the motel room, the first thing he did was make
love to her. Diane still couldn't walk and Bob carried her
everywhere. Often he carried her into the bathroom and
would get so excited holding her that by the time she
needed him to carry her back to the bed, he'd lay her
down carefully and then fall all over her.

Bob loved Diane body and soul by then. Even narcotics had never brought him the pleasure and pure satisfac-

tion that Diane did back then. He often wondered later just why he hadn't given up his use of narcotics and settled down with Diane and tried to do the right thing. It just didn't work out that way, Bob thought, although he also kind of figured he knew the reason why. It was because every time he'd ever tried to do the right thing, insurmountable events had promptly risen up to block his good intentions. It was uncanny. If he got out of the penitentiary and actually did show up at a job, the job would somehow just up and dissolve. And if it wasn't one thing, it was another. If the whole outfit he worked for didn't walk out on strike, his parole officer would start hanging around until he bugged Bob into quitting. And if that didn't happen, then he'd get rousted by some overzealous narcotics cop and end up spending a few days in jail, thus blowing whatever situation he had going.

Those kinds of things never happened to him while he was doing wrong. Then everything came to him as though served on a silver platter. In fact, theft, robbery, burglary, almost anything illegal came so easily to Bob that he finally accepted the fact that that was him, that someone up there in the heavens for some insane reason willed it that way, and that no matter what he did, that was the way it was going to be. Sometimes Bob tossed around the idea that perhaps the devil was his overlord, that he looked out for old Bob in all situations and only let him get caught and punished when Bob did something old Satan objected to. Hell, it was a good theory, as good as the ones those Bible thumpers insisted on telling you. Who knew for sure? No one really seemed to, and it was such a mishmash, life was, such a web of intrigue that

Bob didn't even try to figure it out anymore. He accepted his role in life, that of a drug addict and thief. That was Bob and he was good at it. In fact, he was one of the few dope-fiend thieves he knew who could actually afford an old lady. He knew lots of junkies who couldn't, because even if a woman didn't use dope herself, she had to live, and everything most of those guys got a hold of went straight into their arms. Or if she did use dope, but wasn't a prostitute or thief—so she could hold up her end or maybe even carry her old man—then she was alone, because dope fiends really didn't need the comforts of a woman, even if they could afford to keep one around.

Bob sighed. He really did hate to lose Diane after all these years. She had been good to him. She didn't stand around sniveling when nothing could be gained by acting that way. Instead, she got out and went to work. And she always stuck with her man, even if she was sick and stranded with him somewhere. She always stuck it out. And his thing was her thing, as long as it entailed stealing and using narcotics. You couldn't ask for a better working partner, Bob thought. She'd spit in a cop's eye in a minute. She was virtually fearless in all respects.

Bob grinned as he thought of the time she decided to go straight. She had begun changing her reasoning and loyalties during her first prison term. She'd gotten into one of those group counseling sessions on a regular basis. All the rest of the women in that group were horribly bitter. It was all men's fault. A terrible, dirty, lecherous man had gotten every one of them into their present predicament by some deceitful manner or other. And so Diane began thinking back to how Bob had indoctrinated her into the world of narcotics. She remembered how she had first refused to have anything to do with dope. She would go along for the ride, maybe even share in the use of stolen money. But no dope, thanks anyway. But then somewhere, somehow, it had begun. She had started it. It was a little fuzzy how it had all come to pass. But it had happened, there was no question of that.

In prison, Diane began to believe the group's doctrine with all her heart. Men, they were no damn good for anything. They were always in the driver's seat, and for some reason, they always took advantage of the opposite sex, always held their thumbs down on them, kept the pressure on and always got their own goddamn way. Soon, Diane stopped writing to Bob and even had him taken off the institution mailing list. And then she began to hate him. When she got out, she looked around and found herself a nice, placid fellow whose only dream was to have a livable home to go along with a wife and kids.

Diane ate it all up for a while. She even ribbed herself into believing that she found pleasure in the everyday tasks of changing diapers, doing the wash, cooking supper, and all the other little homey things that went along with her new life. She no doubt would have changed back anyway of her own accord, as her enthusiasm for such a role had a short fuse. But one Saturday morning her husband stayed home with the children while she drove to the local launderette with the weekly wash. And no sooner had she begun to stuff all the dirty clothes, properly separated, into the washing machines, than in walked Bob with another thief. They had a gadget that enabled them to beat the coin changers. And when Bob saw Diane bending over her dirty clothes and throwing

them into the washers, he started to laugh. He laughed
until he was staggering around the foul-smelling, con-
crete-floored room, until his stomach ached and the
tears flooded down his cheeks.

He had heard about the changes Diane had gone
through at the penitentiary, and at the time he took it
stoically enough. What the hell, he had figured, you can't
blame people for wanting changes that they hope will
better their lives. And he had accepted the fact that he
had lost her and that he'd probably never see her again.
And then to find her like this, in her old housedress, in
her flat, scuffed shoes, with her hair in her face and no
makeup, it was just too much, he couldn't contain himself. This is what she had so drastically changed her life
for. Bob couldn't even entertain the thought of anyone
giving up what she had had to accept this, especially
Diane.

Diane stood her ground. She placed her hands on her
now plump hips and just glared back at Bob. He was the
man she detested above all others, the one who had
almost ruined her whole life.

Bob just kept on laughing. Actually, he didn't know
what to say. He didn't want to hurt her; hell, he loved
her, stringy hair and all, and it was kind of funny, especially if you had an odd sense of humor like Bob's in the
first place. Things that others thought were tragic often
caused Bob to smile or maybe to snicker. He might laugh
for a week over some fellow thief's fall through a roof
that gave the poor bastard a broken leg and got him
caught in the bargain. Bob's life was so full of futile,
never-ending tragedies that should he begin to cry over
them, he would have to cry forever. So he even laughed

at his own plight. In fact, he was usually the first to laugh at himself, although he laughed at the plight of others just as readily.

Now his laughing made Diane furious. But when he left, still laughing, Diane couldn't think of anything else but him and the life they had shared. She brooded on it the whole time the washers and dryers were thrashing the clothes around. She thought of how she had never had to do any goddamn wash when she was with him, chiefly because it was easier to shoplift more clothes or trade some low-grade narcotics to other shoplifters than it was to wash, dry, and pack the old ones around. And it wasn't long before Diane began to see things in a different light.

Diane had gone to the launderette that day a bedraggled, harried housewife with nothing on her mind but dirty clothes and dirty kids. But when she returned home a couple of hours later, she was a tiger. Her spirit had returned. She laughed instead of carrying around a frown or looking as if she were on the verge of tears. And once home with the clothes clean and ready to absorb yet another layer of filth, she plunked herself down in a chair and promptly told her husband that from now on, he could do the wash if he wanted it done, and he could do the cooking and housecleaning, and that if he wanted to have more children, then he could find someone else to have them by, because she was sick and tired of the whole stinking mess.

Three days later she left her pathetic home and began hanging around the places where Bob was likely to turn up sooner or later. She hung around for a week before she ran into him, and when she finally saw him, she stepped right up and slapped him across the face as hard as she could, and then announced, "That's for laughing at me, you bastard!"

Bob started laughing again, but now he was laughing with her instead of against her.

She draped her arms around his neck and stood on her tiptoes and whispered, "Need another hand, junkie?"

And Bob came back, "Sure, baby, who doesn't need another hand?"

And so it was. Diane was back, never to stray again, unless, of course, Bob got put away for a while and then Diane only strayed for convenience's sake, to satisfy her needs and accommodate his as well. She never again forgot Bob and she constantly tried to accommodate his slightest whim when he was inside and unable to provide for himself. Diane was regarded by all who knew her in the dope-fiend criminal world as a boss old lady.

Bob stretched out again in the bus's uncomfortable seat and began thinking about pharmacies in general, all the ones he had hit and some of the choicer ways he had dreamed up to take them. Years ago, back in the fifties, wrassling pharmacies was a cinch. All you had to do was declare some obscure kind of emergency and ask to use the druggist's phone, or even the bathroom, anything to get behind the drug counter, before a partner moved in to grab the pharmacist and hold him in the main part of the store. Or sometimes Bob would go in as a telephone lineman, claiming that something was wrong with the phone. And when that wore out, he'd climb the sides or even onto the roofs of the drugstores and make sure the phone was out of order. Then there was the pharmaceutical salesman pitch. A guy had to have a good line of lingo to handle that one, though. And in extreme cases Bob had even had someone act drunk and drive through the front plate glass, and while everyone was up there all excited and raving, he'd dive. Nowadays, though, it seemed as if they weren't giving anything away. You had to come up with something original, like the young woman with the fit and exposed crotch. It seemed as though even if the pharmacists knew it was a diversion they went for it anyway, perhaps because they just couldn't quite believe that anyone would go to those lengths to beat them, or maybe because they never imagined such a thing could happen to them.

Then there was the upsets, the times he'd been caught in the act. Jesus, Bob thought, remembering one occasion when he'd been kneeling in front of the narcotics drawer loading his pockets and a pharmacist had come out of nowhere to haul off and kick him in the rear. Bob's lowered head rammed the cabinets and he toppled to the floor half conscious and moaning while the pharmacist completed the act by kicking Bob in any unguarded area he could find.

Diane, who had been discussing diaphragm fits with the other pharmacist in the store's main area, heard the blows and grunts and saw Bob's assailant, but not Bob. That was enough. She didn't wait for confirmation that her man was in trouble. She grabbed a bottle of shampoo and fired it at the attacker. It missed, but when it shattered against some other bottles behind the pharmacist's head, he looked up, just in time to duck a second bottle. Diane then tossed a third, missing again. About this time the first pharmacist, momentarily baffled into inaction by the bottle pitching, leaped forward to grab her arms.

Diane ducked and directed a fourth bottle at this closer target, connecting with the man's chest. The pharmacist backed away, looking amazed and rubbing his chest. Diane then aimed for him again and lobbed another one in the general direction of the counter.

Diane's pharmacist now began to get braver, no doubt motivated by fear that she would wreck the joint. Diane was trying to. She scooped up several articles and showered him with them as he lunged for her. She sidestepped him and pulled over a rack of display items. Her pharmacist attempted to jump over the debris and continue his attack, but one foot landed on a spinning bottle and he crashed full length on his back in the middle of the mess.

While he lay there groaning, Diane renewed her attack on the second pharmacist. She closed the distance between her and the counter so the man could not duck so easily and began barraging him with whatever came to hand. He frantically tried to use the telephone for help, but she managed a direct hit before he got the number dialed. So he gave up and fled to the back room, while Diane charged around the counter and tried to drag Bob outside. He soon came out of his stupor enough to navigate with her aid. And when they finally got to the car, the first thing Diane asked was, "Did you get any blues?"

Bob smiled to himself and looked around the bus, wondering if any of these other passengers had ever been in such an insane situation. Not likely, he surmised, but then, one just couldn't look at people and tell much about them anymore. It took all kinds to make up a world and just because people were elderly and looked respectable, it didn't mean they were or always had been. Take that darling old grandma over there, for example, Bob speculated, knitting away so fastidiously. To look at her one wouldn't think she had ever done anything in her whole life but raise her children and her children's children. But who knows, she might have been a hooker and a bawdy dancer up in Alaska during the gold rush. She could have been a spy for Germany during the First World War. She could have murdered fourteen people and skinned them and eaten them for all anyone knew. But right now, right this minute, she was a darling old grandma and most likely that's all she'd ever been.

However, Bob had run into many older people in his life who weren't nice and proper just because they were old or looked and acted that way. Now, take that guy in the second seat, way up there. He was half crocked now, rumpled and as grubby as any bum on skid row. And who was he? He could very easily have been an upstanding businessman just a few years ago. Plenty of the bums and winos of today were just that not so long ago. Or he might have been a hit man for the Mafia. Bob grinned at his fantasizing, because if the old boy had been a hit man, he sure had everyone fooled now. But then again, wasn't that usually the case? How long would a hit man for the Mafia survive if he looked and acted the part like they do in the movies?

Bob had to smile again at his thoughts, for he had known many a dope fiend, usually young, who just had to have everyone in the world know it. They played their parts to a tee. That seemed to be as much a part of their kick, or even more, than the euphoria produced by the drugs. And then they wondered why the cops always bugged them and constantly shook them down. "The goddamn snitches," they'd swear. Snitches, hell, Bob thought. They snitched on themselves most of the time. They were like a burglar traveling to a score wearing a dark turtleneck sweater, black tennis shoes, black gloves, and carrying a crowbar over the shoulder. It looked fine on TV but it just didn't work out well in real life. There wasn't a cop in any city in the nation who would give you a pass if he spotted you heading down the road dressed like that. And there wasn't a narco detective who wouldn't look you over very carefully should he spot you standing downtown at the bus station leaning up against a wall with your eyes closed, leisurely scratching and rubbing your body with heavenly bliss written all over your mug.

The bus ride took eight hours, and by the time Bob arrived at the coast city he was sick. Still, he checked out all his luggage, caught a cab, rode to a broken-down hotel, and checked in before he got out his outfit and fixed up.

The next morning he got up early, looked up the city's methadone center in the phone book, and walked to it. He was there when they opened that morning. He followed them in and sat down in the waiting room. Presently an older woman came in, looked him over, went into her office, and then returned and asked, "Well, young man, what can we do for you this morning?"

Bob looked up and grinned. "I want to sign up for your withdrawal program," he said.

The woman smiled back and said, "I see. And when was the last time you took whatever you use?"

"Last night."

"Are you going to get violently sick today, then? You

realize that to get right on the withdrawal program you have to be in the third stage of withdrawal, sweating, stomach cramps, chills, temperature, and so on?"

"Yes."

"Have you ever been on either the maintenance or withdrawal program before?"

"No."

"I see. Now, how long have you been addicted to whatever you're on now?"

"This time?"

"Then this isn't your first time withdrawing?"

"No, but it's my first time withdrawing on methadone."

"I see. Well, how long have you been using drugs altogether?"

"All my life."

"All your life?"

Skepticism showed on the woman's face.

"Well, since I've been twelve or thirteen I've been using narcotics. I guess you could say that was all my life."

"How old are you now?"

"Thirty-five."

"Why do you want to quit now, after all that time? I'd think you'd be inclined to go right on with it. Why quit now?"

Bob shrugged and grinned. "I don't know, curiosity I guess," he said. "I just thought I'd try it."

"Are you serious?" the woman asked, smiling back. "I mean, we get a lot of guys and gals coming up here just trying to get in on a new kick and that's not what we're here for. We're here for people that just have nowhere else to turn."

"Well, lady, you just found you one of those people that ain't got any other way to turn, so give me a jolt and let me go on my merry way."

"Oh, my, it's not that easy, young man. You've got all kinds of paperwork to fill out. You've got a doctor's examination to go through, and then maybe, just maybe, we'll help you out. You've got to get sick first, too, you know."

Bob grinned. "Don't you worry your head a bit about that, ma'am. I'll get sick. I'll get so sick you won't be able to refuse me. Just you watch and see."

Bob spent the day on the couch in the waiting room. Along about noon his nose began to run. By two o'clock he was shaking violently. At three his stomach began to cramp and the fits of sneezing began and his clothes were damp with perspiration. At four o'clock they finally called in a doctor to examine him. And at six he stumbled out with a dose of methadone in him. He was still sick and shaking like a leaf, but he knew that within a half hour it would all be over and he'd be able to function enough to make it through the night on his own, and that was half the battle.

Returning to his room, he lay on the bed and stared at the wall. Soon his shaking body began to relax and the terrible weakness that invades one's body during withdrawal began to ebb.

The next day he returned to the methadone center. After receiving his dose, he was ushered into a small office to talk with the woman he had seen the previous morning.

"Hello, Mr. Hughes, my name is Miss Simpson, and I am your counselor for as long as you're with us. You know, Mr. Hughes, when I first saw you yesterday, I didn't really take you seriously. In fact, I even speculated that perhaps you might be one of those investigator types who nose around to see how we handle our programs. I was quite amazed when I read the doctor's report. I think you're probably getting the biggest dose that we have ever handed out here."

Bob smiled and said nothing.

"Well, hmm, let me see now, I wanted to ask you a few things before we go on much further. Let's see, are you married?"

"Yes."

"Where is your wife?"

"I don't know."

"Hmm, I see. Do you have any children?"

"My wife does. I don't."

"Do you have a job?"

"No."

"Hmm, I see. And when is the last time you held down a job?"

"Never."

"Never? You mean to say that you have never had a job?"

"Nope."

"Well, how do you live? Are you rich or something?"

"No, I've just been scuffling along. Just an old gutter tramp, so to speak."

"Do you have a social security number?"

"No."

"Hmm, I see. Mr. Hughes, have you ever been convicted of a felony?"

"Yeah, a couple times."

"What were they, what kind of felonies were you convicted of?"

"Oh, burglary, robbery, possession, grand theft, stuff like that."

"Hmm. And how much time have you spent in prison, Mr. Hughes?"

"Oh, I don't know, fifteen years, more or less, I suppose."

"Well, then, you haven't been an addict all your life then, have you, Mr. Hughes?"

"What do you mean?"

"I mean you could hardly have been an addict in prison, now, could you, Mr. Hughes?"

"Why not?"

"Do you mean to sit there and tell me that you were addicted to drugs while in prison?"

"Well, not all the time. But I used all the time I was inside, and I suppose I was addicted some of the time. I mean, what do you want, lady, my life story? Well, I'll tell it to you. I was a junkie. I liked dope, I liked the lifestyle. I was on top of it all. You don't see my kind of people, because my kind of people don't come down here and beg dope. They go out and get it, and if they miss, they go to jail and then they kick alone without nothing in some investigating tank. Well, that was me, but I thought maybe I'd change, so I came down here to see you people to see if maybe a guy like me could change and all it seems you people want to do is question my authenticity and ridicule me for the way I am. What can I say? What will make you get off my back? You don't have to change me. I came here, me, I came right down to this place and I said will you please help me get rid of this habit I got. You don't have to counsel me. The courts didn't send me here. I came myself. If I didn't want to quit, I wouldn't be here, but I am, so obviously I do. So what's the hassle?"

Miss Simpson held up her hand. "I'm sorry, Mr. Hughes," she said. "I don't want to hassle you, and believe me, I am not trying to ridicule you. It's just that for someone as naive as me, your story sounds kind of fantastic. And I do need to know all this or I wouldn't be asking it. It isn't that I have a morbid curiosity, Mr. Hughes. All this is required. I'm sorry if it seems unnecessary."

"That's all right," Bob grinned, settling back in his chair. "I just get kind of excited when someone asks me a question and then looks skeptical about my answer."

Miss Simpson smiled at Bob's attempts to apologize. "Well, Mr. Hughes, are you now going to try to find some type of employment?"

"Yeah, I guess I'll have to find something."

"Do you have something in mind, some friend who may be willing to give you work or something of that nature?"

"Nope. I don't know a living soul that would help me in any way."

"Hmm, I see. Well, it just so happens that I have a friend down at the state employment office, and I'm sure that if I sent you down there, she'd try to get you something. Would you like that? Would you take a job if she could get one for you?"

"Yeah, that would be all right."

Then they sat in silence. The moments seemed to grow into minutes. Finally Miss Simpson asked, "What happened, Mr. Hughes? Did your wife leave you?"

Bob sat up in his chair and thought for a while, then said, "No, I don't think you could say that. Actually, I guess I left her."

"Is she an addict also?"

Again Bob mulled over the question before answering. "I don't know. Maybe she is. I never thought to ask her."

Miss Simpson looked at Bob oddly. "Well, I guess that's all for today," she announced. "Tomorrow, after you get your dose, why don't you go down to the state employment office and ask for Mrs. Watermaker. She'll be expecting you. I'll call her tonight and we'll see if we can't get you some kind of a job. Oh, Mr. Hughes, do you have any clothes to wear to work?"

Bob looked down at his clothes and then back at Miss Simpson. He shrugged and said, "I suppose so."

"What I mean, Bob, is that if we get you a job digging a ditch somewhere, you can hardly go out on the job wearing slacks and a sport jacket."

"Why not?"

"Why not? Well, yes, I see what you mean. Oh yes, one other thing. Do you have a place to stay?"

"I do right now. I haven't got much money, though, and my rent will be up in a few days, so I guess I'd better get that job right away."

"Hmm, I see. Would you care to come into a halfway house? I could probably help you with that also."

Bob thought it over for a few moments and then shook his head. "No, I don't think so, Miss Simpson. Let's see if I can't make it on my own."

"Bob, about this employment situation. Have you ever thought about becoming a counselor and helping other addicts with their problems? Oh, you'd need some training and some counseling yourself first, but don't you think that would be a worthwhile project, helping others with the same problems that you have had? If anyone should know about them, it's someone like you."

"No, I don't think so, Miss Simpson. I don't think it would be a worthwhile project at all," Bob said without hesitation.

"Well, for heaven's sake, why not?" she said, looking slightly aghast.

"Well, to begin with, no one, and I mean no one, can talk a junkie out of using, so all your counseling is just wasted words and you might as well flush them down the toilet. I mean, you people haven't got nothing to offer a junkie that's any better than what he's got. What can you give him? Nothing but empty advice that works for you because you ain't a junkie. A junkie needs his thing nine times out of ten just to be able to live with himself. He needs it just like a diabetic needs insulin. How are you going to sit and talk a diabetic out of using insulin? You aren't. Oh, you might get to a weak one, but even if you do, the poor sucker's probably going to get sick and eventually die, and Miss Simpson, that's just about what's going to happen to your junkie without his stuff. Oh, he might not die, but he may as well."

"Well, Bob, you seem to be doing all right. I mean, you're on methadone. But I just have this funny feeling about you. I feel you're going to get off drugs and then stay off them. I can't pin down exactly why I have come to that conclusion, but I suppose it has something to do with your attitude, the fact that you don't lie and try to tell us what we want to hear. Tell me, Bob, why are you here?"

Bob laughed, thought for a moment, and said, "You wouldn't believe me if I told you, Miss Simpson. I'm sorry, but that's the absolute truth. You just wouldn't believe me, and even if you did, it would just confuse you, and even if it didn't, it wouldn't help you with anyone else."

"Hmm, I see. Well, tell me, Bob, if you can, why did you use narcotics?"

Bob sat and squirmed in his chair. He considered the question for a long time, looking out the office window. Finally, he turned back to the woman and began, "That's really a tough question. I may think I know the answer, and then maybe I don't. But even if I did, I don't think I could put it in words. About all I can do is give you a similarity, and the nearest I can come to it is this: When you ask a dope fiend why he uses, it's just about like asking a normal person why he likes sex. And I suppose different people will come up with different answers, ranging from it just feels good to I can't resist the urge, to it's all part of love, to I only do it to have children. Miss Simpson, a dope fiend will give you just about the same answers, with the exception perhaps of the last one. I've yet to hear a dope fiend claim he shot dope in an attempt to have children, but I've heard all the rest. And I've even heard dope fiends claim that good old heroin is better than any woman they ever had. Now, I've never had any heroin that was quite that good, but give me a couple of sixteenths of Dilaudid mixed with four or five fifteen-milligram tabs of Desoxyn and I'd walk over the damndest pile of naked movie starlets you ever saw just to get at it."

"You know, Bob," Miss Simpson said, smiling. "I think you're probably the first dope fiend that we've had in here who really attempted to tell the whole, unmitigated truth. Perhaps not the truth, but the way you really feel, and the one thing that I can't understand is, if you feel as strongly attracted toward narcotics as you say, why you came down here to take this withdrawal program in the first place. I mean, Bob, it just doesn't quite make sense."

Bob stood up and stretched. "Miss Simpson, I think you'll find if you work here long enough that few things will make sense to you. There never was a junkie alive that made good sense. They are not exactly noted for that. They *feel*, Miss Simpson, and everything surrounding their whole trip is felt, and it either feels good or it feels bad. Did you ever stop to think, Miss Simpson, that some people may just feel so bad all the time that they got to have something to make them feel better, and without that life just ain't worth the effort? Did you ever stop to think that some people hurt so much naturally, are so depressed with life and their role in it, that they can't stand it without an antidote that will bring them some kind of relief? And, Miss Simpson, you can talk to them for years and you may con them out of it for a while, but sooner or later they are going to get hold of something, maybe not dope, maybe booze, maybe glue, maybe gasoline, maybe just a gunshot in the head, or gas, maybe even religion, but something to relieve them of the pressures of their everyday lives. Oh, I know, Miss Simpson, that their troubles may well be imaginary. Nine

chances out of ten they are, without a doubt, but that
don't make them any less real to the person who is imagining them."

There was not much more to add to that, so Miss
Simpson told him he could go. Bob returned to the hotel
that afternoon and stayed in the lobby, sitting on an old
couch and watching the people pass by in the street.
He'd been there for about an hour when an older man
hobbled out of the elevator and limped into the lobby
room and also took a seat. Bob recognized the old guy
and called out, "How you making it, Tom?"

The man looked up and squinted over his glasses.
Finally his face lit up. "Well, hi, Bob. I didn't even recognize you. How are you doing?"

"Not too goddamn good," Bob said, shrugging and
grinning. "Got myself on the methadone withdrawal
program. Thought I might try to kick the dragon out of
bed for a while."

Tom grinned back, although it was obvious he was in
pain. "Is that right? Jesus, I just got out of the joint last
week. I went down to that methadone center first thing,
right off the bat and gave them my spiel, and they don't
want to go for it. I guess they figure an old duffer like me,
he ain't no kind of threat no more, and the bastards, they
ain't giving nothing away for free. Hell, if I'd have
knowed that, I'd have stayed in prison. I could get more
up there on the giveaway side from my friends than I can
out here."

Bob shook his head at Tom's misery. "You mean they
wouldn't put you on methadone, Tom? Hell, you used to
be the most terrible dope fiend on the coast. Jesus, if they

gave it to anybody, I'd of thought they'd give it to you. What are you going to do now?"

"Oh, I don't know, Bob. They'll probably be stuffing cotton in my ass any day now. I know I ain't got long to go. I'd just like to make one more run, get me one more oil burner going before I check out. Shit, I thought this methadone thing was going to be the ticket for me. A feller just can't depend on anything no more. Hell, they'll give it to those snot-nosed kids by the carload, but I guess they figure that them kids is dangerous. They took one look at me and said come back when you're dirty, old man. You got to have three dirty urines and a doctor's examination before you can get on the methadone program, and hell, I ain't got the money even to pay a doctor for a prescription, even if I could talk one into writing for me."

"Jesus, that's too bad, Tom. I'll tell you what, though. I'm pretty tight right now with one of the counselors down there, and tomorrow, first thing right off the bat, I'll bring up your case. Maybe I can help some. I ain't promising nothing, but I'll try."

Old Tom looked up in gratitude. He licked his dry lips and said, "Jesus, Bob, thanks. I sure would appreciate it if you can help me. Tell them I ain't going to be with them long anyhow, and I just got to get something going for myself. Hell, I was just now sitting here thinking maybe I'd go down the street to the nearest druggy, put my hand in my pocket like I had a gun, and try to con them out of their stuff. The only thing is, I can't get around too good and I'd probably have a hell of a time getting back here to the hotel. I'll tell you what, though, Bob. If you can line us up a gun and transportation and

drive for me, I'll run on in and get any joint you point
out, and if I don't make it back out, all you got to do is
drive on off. I won't blame you for doing that, neither."

"Tom, you're too much." Bob grinned back. "How
goddamn old are you, anyway? You got to be at least
ninety. Hell, you was an old duffer when I was just a kid.
You stay out of those drugstores, Tom. Hell, that's a kid's
game and you know it. I'll get you on that methadone
program or I'll get you something. Come on, come on up
to my room. I want to show you something."

They walked to the elevator. Bob had to keep stopping
and turning back to wait for the stooped, limping Tom.
Good God, Bob thought to himself, if he ever does get
into a drugstore, he'll probably have a heart attack and
fall out before he gets back outside.

When they entered Bob's room, Bob settled Tom in
the room's only chair and went down the hall to find his
stash. When he returned, he threw the old man a bundle
wrapped in a sock. "Here, knock your lights out. It ain't
much, but it should hold you for a few days. There's an
outfit in there too."

Bob left again to get a glass of water, and he walked
back in to find Tom with the outfit ready to go and a
sixteenth in a spoon. His hands were shaking so badly
that he could hardly keep it all together and the tears ran
down his cheeks and glistened against the gray pallor of
his skin. "Jesus, Bob," he said, "I don't know how to
thank you. I didn't know what I was going to do. This is
all I live for anymore, you know, and I was stumped,
completely stumped. I just couldn't figure any way to get
well, and hell, no one gives stuff away anymore, not like
in the old days. Boy, I wish you'd have been with me

then, Bob. The pharmacies were real fat then. I remember back in the thirties, when a man had to be careful and
maybe make two trips into one of them poison shops just
to haul all the stuff in them out, and I mean good stuff,
class A, not this crap that all these kids fool around with
nowadays. Many's the time I thought I'd sprained my
back, humping out of one of those joints loaded down
like I was. Things just seem to get worse all the time
nowadays, don't they, Bob? Things always seem to
change for the worse. I've often wondered why that is."

"I don't know, Tom, but I know what you mean," Bob
said, grinning and shaking his head.

The next day Bob went to the state employment office
and found Mrs. Watermaker, a middle-aged, roly-poly,
forever-smiling lady.

"Why, you must be Miss Simpson's boy," she said.
"I've heard all about you. Now, what kind of a job do you
think you can handle?"

Bob shrugged. "Damned if I know, to be truthful with
you. You just point one out and I'll give it one heck of a
try."

"Have you ever drilled any holes before?"

Bob looked back at her quizzically. "What do you
mean?"

"You know, drill holes. Like with a drill, like in a machine shop where they make parts for different things."

"Oh, that kind of drilling." Bob smiled. "Yeah, I guess
you could say I've drilled a few holes in my time. That
sounds like just the job for me. Where do I go?"

"Now, wait a minute. You have to fill out some paperwork first. And don't you want to know what they pay?"

"Oh, yeah. What do they pay?"

"Well, I believe they only start you out at the minimum wage, but if you do all right and show any initiative at all, they'll soon give you a raise, probably after the first thirty days."

Bob thanked Mrs. Watermaker and headed for the machine shop. When he found it, he entered and looked around. He had never seen such machinery before. Everything seemed dirty, in a way, and the screech of metal being cut away by high-speed cutters assailed his ears. Presently an older man in overalls approached Bob and asked, "Can I help you, son?"

"Yeah. I'm supposed to report here for work in the morning and I thought I'd come on down and look the place over. Sure seems like you're doing a lot of work here."

The older man smiled. "You must be the new driller then. Have you ever done this kind of work before?"

"No, to be truthful, I haven't," Bob said, figuring that any attempt to lie would prove ridiculous.

The older man looked Bob over carefully, then said, "Well, I guess you're honest, anyway. And there ain't really a whole lot to your job to begin with. I mean, there is, and then again there isn't. A good driller is really hard to find. Not just anyone can drill a hole. Oh, they can punch one through all right, but that ain't drilling. You got to get the feel of it. You got to be able to hold to tolerances, know your speeds and what have you, but it isn't nothing you can't learn if you got the knack for drilling holes. And if you do, you'll catch on to the rest soon enough. And if you don't, I'll know right off, and then we'll have to let you go. But hell, I'll try you. You just get here tomorrow morning along about eight o'clock and we'll give you a tryout then."

Bob smiled back. "Thanks. I'll be here tomorrow at eight."

Bob then walked to the methadone maintenance center. He had to wait an hour to see Miss Simpson. Then she came out of her office and smiled at Bob. "Well, I hear you got a job."

Bob stood and smiled back. "Well, not exactly. The guy's going to give me a trial run in the morning, but I don't know if I can handle it or not. I'll try, don't get me wrong. It's just that everything looks so strange and complex down there. Anyway, what I want to see you about is this friend of mine. He's a real old man, probably on his last legs right now. He just got out of the joint and he's hurting bad. He's been a dope fiend all his life and I think the only reason he took a parole and came out was to get on the methadone program that he's heard so much about. He ain't got a soul looking out for him and I really do feel sorry for the old boy. I was just wondering if you could stick your oar in someplace and get him on it."

Miss Simpson held up her hands in protest. "Bob!"

Bob went right on with his spiel. "Lady, this guy at one time was the king of the dopers here on the coast. At one time he owned hotels, cab lines, night clubs, he was a hell of a gambler. Him and his wife, Sally, they must have shot more than a million bucks' worth of dope in their arms. They always was good people, Miss Simpson. They took care of anybody that needed help."

"What happened to his wife?"

"She got killed by a car while she was crossing the street up on Broadway a couple of years ago."

"Well, Bob, I'd like to help your friend out, really I would, but to begin with, I'm not in that end of it. I'm working strictly on withdrawal cases. And even if I did go beyond my scope and speak up for your friend, there are certain requirements, policies, and laws controlling these programs. We just can't give anyone methadone, just because they think they might like some. These programs are set up for a specific type of individual, one who is already addicted and who needs help. Also, I just can't have you out there running around digging up customers, so to speak. It just isn't done."

Bob sighed. "Miss Simpson, are you going to make me go out and wrassle some drugstore to get the stuff, so that he can pass your requirements? Now, I'll do it if I have to. This guy isn't the normal everyday gutter type. This old man has got a lot of class. He's old and hurting now and he don't look like much, but I want you to know that if I have to, I'll go out and get that old man some stuff."

Miss Simpson looked pained. "Bob, if I do help you out now, how often is this going to happen? I mean, you're not going to be coming in here every other week or so with another good guy who just wants to get loaded, are you?"

"I hope not, princess," Bob said, smiling. "I don't usually get involved in this kind of thing and I wouldn't be involved now if this particular case wasn't so pathetic. I mean, if this guy had the money to go to any doctor other than the welfare ones, they'd no doubt write a narcotics prescription for him, just for his pain. The old guy's hurting, and not only physically but mentally as well. He needs help bad."

"Okay, Bob, okay, bring him in. I'll talk to him and I'll help him all I can. But I can't promise you anything. Our biggest hurdle is going to be the doctor who examines him. Now, I know most of the doctors who come in here and we're going to have to wait for one of the more sympathetic ones before we run your friend through. Then there's the dirty urines. He's got to come up with three dirty urines. I'll leave that up to you."

"What if I pee in that bottle? Would they know the difference?"

"I'm sure I don't know, Bob. You'll have to ask someone else and I don't want to know anything about that end of it either. Perhaps you had better go hold your friend's hand, because if he's as bad off as you've made him out to be, he no doubt needs you."

"You're all right, princess," Bob grinned. "You're really all right. I wonder why it is, you always find the best people in the places you'd least expect to."

"Go on, Bob, get out of here," Miss Simpson said, looking around her. "I've got work to do."

When Bob reached the hotel that evening he went right up to old Tom's room and knocked. Then he waited a few minutes while Tom painfully got out of bed and slowly made his way to the door.

Bob entered and noticed a terrible smell. It was a musky, heavy odor, which he somehow associated with death and dying. It took Tom a long time to get eased back on his bed. When he finally got settled, Bob announced, "Well, I think we got things going our way, old thing. I talked to my lady friend down at the methadone center and she's going to do all she can to help you. But we still got to come up with three dirty urines and get you past the examining doctor. She's going to pick the doctor and if need be, I'm going to pee in the bottle for you. So it looks like we're all set. However, things could still go wrong. A lot is going to depend on what you say and how you present yourself down there. I'll get Miss Simpson to coach you some, and now we got to get us some kind of transportation to get you down there. How in hell are we going to manage that? Even if you do get on, how are you going to get down there to get your daily dose?"

Tom grinned, almost crying at the same time. "Jesus, Bob, I sure do want to thank you for helping me like this. And don't you get to worrying about how I'm going to get down there. I'll get down there some way. If they got my dope down there, I'll get down there to get it."

Bob wished old Tom luck and backed out the door. As he walked toward his own room, he wondered idly what it was about helping others that made a guy feel so good. He couldn't come up with an answer, so he dismissed it from his mind and unlocked and opened his door. There sat Detective Gentry, lounging in the chair.

Bob didn't say anything or give any indication he had seen Gentry. He closed the door, locked it, took off his coat and hung it in the closet. Finally Gentry asked, "What're you going to do, Bob, just shine me on?"

Bob turned and grinned at the big detective. "Oh, it's you. I thought it was my kid sister sitting there."

Gentry ignored the remark. "You didn't stay gone long, Bob. What happened?"

"Nothing happened," Bob said, shrugging his shoulders. He plopped onto the bed and braced his hands behind his head. "Things just didn't work out, so I gave up and came back."

"I hear you're on the methadone withdrawal program now. Is that right? Now, you don't think that's going to keep Halamer from jumping on you, do you, Bob?"

"To tell the truth, I hadn't given it much thought."

"Well, Bob, I want to tell you something, warn you, so to speak. Halamer's mad. He lost his gold badge, you know, over that little fracas. He's now working traffic out in the north end. Don't go out there, Bob. Steer clear of him if you can. As far as I know, he doesn't know you're back in town yet, and I'm damn sure not going to tell him, mainly because I don't want to see him get into any more trouble. And, Bob. He's made so damn many threats, he's told so many people just what he's going to do to you should you ever come back, that he's almost going to have to hurt you now. Either that or leave town himself, and I just can't quite see him doing that."

"What about the Strangler? How's he feeling about the whole affair?"

"Don't you worry about Trousinski, Bob. He's not really mean. He just does his job the best way he knows how. Oh, he holds no love for you, don't get me wrong. However, he's not going to go out of his way to get you either. But Halamer will."

Gentry and Bob were quiet for a few moments. Finally Bob coughed and said, "Well, I don't know what to tell you. I got a job, you know. I start work tomorrow."

"Yeah, that's what I heard," Gentry grunted. "What happened out there in the sticks, Bob? Where's Diane?"

Bob shrugged. "You know how whimsical women are. She finally found another dude to chase after, and down the road she went, chasing after him."

Gentry chewed on that for a while and then said, "You

know what, Bob? I've known you and Diane since we were all kids, and I find that rather hard to believe."

Gentry then slowly rose from the chair. "I'll see you around, Bob," he said. "And I sincerely hope you make out on that job you've got and straighten up a bit. However, I've been around dope fiends for a long time and I find all this rather hard to believe. There's a gimmick in it someplace, Bob, and it will all come to light sooner or later, so you just stay out of Halamer's way in the meantime."

At eight o'clock the next morning, Bob showed up at the machine shop. The overall-wearing man of the day before met him just inside the door and took him over to a section of the shop that housed nothing but drill presses of varying sizes and shapes.

"This is the drilling section, Bob," the man said. "By the way, I'm the shop foreman. My name's Henry Zitten, but everybody just calls me Hank. Now, your immediate section lead man will be here any minute. He's a good old guy and he'll help you all he can. You just listen to him and you'll do fine."

Just then a small, sly-looking older fellow came hurrying toward them.

"That's him now. Clarence, this is Bob. He's going to work with you today. He admits he don't know much about this kind of work, so you help him."

Clarence beamed. "That's just the kind of driller I like. It's a whole lot easier trying to teach one that don't know nothing the right way to drill, than it is to try to change somebody who knows it all and has all the bad habits."

Clarence then stuck out his hand. Bob hesitated for a moment. In his world the handshake was a long-abandoned ceremony. Finally he got his hand out there, though, and if Clarence noticed his hesitation he didn't remark about it, as he clamped on and started shaking and talking as if they were war buddies reunited after all these years.

"Is that the clothes you're going to work in?" Clarence asked, after dropping the small talk.

Bob nodded.

"Hell, them's better clothes than I wear to church. What's the matter, son? You just get out of jail or you on the lam?"

And then Clarence winked and grinned even more, as if to say, "If you are, don't worry about me. I won't give you away."

Bob grinned back at Clarence. "You're a smart old duffer, ain't you? I'll bet you've seen the inside of a jail more than once or twice yourself."

"You'd probably win that bet, son," Clarence laughed. "But let's not go into that. We're now talking about you, and I'm your immediate supervisor. What I say goes concerning you, so don't just get too smart alecky."

Bob laughed and added, "I didn't have this here job until ten minutes ago, old thing, and I don't think as easy as this one was to get that I'll have much trouble finding another, so make it easy on yourself."

"Well, you don't seem to scare easy," said Clarence, beaming even more. "I'll say that for ya. Now, if you can just drill a goddamn hole as good as you can pass the buck, you'll be all set."

Bob ran to the hotel during lunch hour and called a taxi to take Tom to the methadone center. He returned to work late and Clarence was waiting on him.

"Good Christ, man," he groused. "First day on the job and you go off and take a two-hour lunch break. You got to be crazy."

"I'm sorry. I had to go back to my room and help this old fellow that lives down the hall get to the doctor."

"Jesus, even I could come up with a better yarn than that," Clarence exclaimed. "You must be telling the truth. Can't the old guy get someone else to help him?"

"Yeah, he probably could, but I had to go with him this first time to introduce him. I'll try and line up someone else to help him down from now on."

Clarence walked away shaking his head. Bob worked the rest of the day and found the work exacting but not hard. Everything had to be just so, and having done none of this before, he had trouble remembering all the advice he had received from Clarence.

That evening Bob lay in his bed pretty much exhausted from his first day's work. He wanted to sleep but he was so keyed up and restless that all he could do was toss and turn. About eleven o'clock someone tapped lightly on his door. Bob got out of bed and stepped to the door. "Who's there?" he called out.

"It's me, Diane."

Bob threw open the door and smiled. Diane stepped in hesitantly and looked around at the room's dismal appearance. She looked shocked. "Jesus, what kind of a dump is this? And where's the female? You might as well trot her out."

"You don't ever change, do you, Diane?" Bob grinned.

"You goddamn right I don't. Why should I?"

Bob shrugged. "I was just remarking on how good you look. I didn't mean nothing by it."

"I'll bet. You're slipperier than an eel, Bob. No one ever catches you off balance because you stay off balance constantly, just to stay on your feet."

"Is that all you got to say?" Bob said, laughing. "Is that why you came up here, or did you just want to see me down and out?"

"You know better than that, Bob. I just wanted to see you, period. How's the methadone thing?"

"Oh, so-so. Got me a job too. I'll bet you never expected to see that."

"No shit!" The shock showed plainly on her face. "Where you working?"

"Oh, down at some machine shop on Western."

"What do you do there?"

"Drill holes."

"Drill holes?"

"Yeah, you know, like the holes that bolts fit into and such."

"Oh yeah? How do you like it?"

"Well, to tell the truth, it's kind of a drag."

"Then you're really serious. You're going to go on with this thing."

"Yeah, I think so, Diane. Sit down, here. Why don't you take off your coat and stay awhile."

"Oh, I can't, Bob, I got people waiting for me down in the car. I just came up to see how you was doing. Here," she said, struggling through her bag and coming up with a small package. "This is from Rick and the rest of us. We kind of thought you might need a taste once in a while."

Bob smiled and took the package. "Thanks, Diane. I sure do appreciate you all thinking of me."

"Bob?"

"Yeah?"

"What happened? What made you turn around that day? Was it me, did I do something wrong? Or was it just that thing with Nadine?"

"No, baby," Bob began, looking grim. "It wasn't you and it wasn't really Nadine's death. It was the hex she threw on us mostly with that silly hat. And then I went and panicked when I looked out into that parking lot and seen all those cop cars. I just knew we were dead and stinking. Everything up till then had gone wrong, with them trying to chase us out of our room and all. I just knew we was going to get busted, and so I started copping deuces. I prayed like I ain't never prayed before. I said, 'God, Devil, Sun, whoever you are up there that controls this whirly-girly, mad, tumbling world, please have pity on us four frightened mortals this day. Please let us get this poor girl's body out of this motel room and on down the road and into the ground so I don't have to spend the rest of my life in prison for something I had no control over. And God, Sun, Satan, if you'll do that for me, I'll show my appreciation by going back to the coast, getting on the methadone program, cleaning up my hand, getting a job, and living the good life.' Well, we got out, and I promised, so here I am."

Diane's eyes were moist. "Are you going to stick to it forever?" she asked.

Bob nodded. "I suppose so. Hell, once a man starts copping deuces he's done for, anyway. Anytime a thief has to go outside his own skill and the luck of the draw and ask for outside help to control the situation, he's done for, anyway. Once I get to depending on begging to get me out of jams, why hell, the next thing you know, I'll

be begging policemen to let me out of jail when they do
get me, and you know what policemen want in return for
favors like that. They want all your friends, and can't you
just see me after begging my way out of jail going around
setting up all my friends? And that's what it would come
to, Diane, and you know it as well as I.

"And then there was that goddamn hex, that hat on
the bed. A thief, he's just like a gambler in some respects.
He's got to have that *edge*. He's got to have Lady Luck
riding on his shoulder. And, Diane, you can be the best
gambler or thief in the world, and if you don't have luck
you're dead, because I don't care how skillfully you play
your cards, you still ain't going to win if all you get is bad
ones. And when you're a thief, and even if you only pick
easy jobs, if you don't have a little luck, something still
can go wrong and usually does. I just couldn't beat that
combination, first a hex and then to find myself copping
deuces. I mean, just imagine a gambler in a high-stakes
game, the cards are dealt and he has a good prospective
hand, all he needs is the ace of spades to have an unbeat-
able hand. So he gets into the pot slowly at first, but soon
he's in so deep that he can't get out, and so everything he
has or will ever hope to have is staked on this one hand of
cards. And then the gambler panics and he starts to pray,
'Please, whoever you are, give me the ace of spades on
the draw and let me win this one hand, and if you do, I'll
never play another hand of cards as long as I live. Please,
just do me this one favor, and I'll go home and work and
take care of my wife and kids.' And he gets it, Diane, he
gets the ace of spades, he wins the hand, and all of a
sudden he realizes that he's actually lost. He's lost all
that he ever really cared about, his way of life gambling

with other men, pitting his skill against their skill, his luck against their luck. He lost it all, because how can he dare go back into another game after making that promise and then getting his prayers answered? It would be impossible, because as a gambler or a thief he knows that he's dependent upon luck, and he gave his away, and he's as good as dead unless he complies with the rules of the game."

Diane sat down on the bed and sighed. "You're crazy, Bob, you are really crazy," she said. "But I see what you mean. Why didn't you say something that day? Why didn't you tell me what it was all about?"

"I couldn't, Diane, I was just sick. I didn't know what to do. I didn't really have it all together in my head. I don't think I could have explained it right then anyway."

"Jesus, Bob, if I had known what it was all about, I'd have come along with you. I thought you were mad at me for falling down in that closet and over things I said."

Bob grinned at the mention of Diane falling down in the closet with Nadine on top of her. "Why don't you go tell your friends you're going to stay the night, and then come back up here and bed down with me for a while?"

"Jesus, I'd like to, Bob," Diane said, lowering her eyes, "but I got another old man now. You remember Bill Snelling? Well, you weren't around, and Bob, you left me, you know. I didn't leave you. So I ran across him and you know how it goes, a girl's got to have someone."

Bob nodded and remained silent.

Diane brightened and said, "We both work for Rick now. Ain't that a gas? There we were, teaching the brat to steal, and now I'm on his crew. Things sure can get screwed around, can't they?"

Bob nodded.

"Jesus, Bob, I'd like to stay the night with you, really I would. Only I'm Bill's old lady now, and you know me, Bob, I might have been a lot of things, but I never was a tramp."

"I'll see you, Diane," Bob said, managing a smile. "You stop back by sometime. It sure was good to see you. And you're really looking good. I sure wish I could go with you and win you back."

Then Bob hustled Diane out the door and waved at her as she headed down the corridor. When she was gone, he closed the door slowly, wandered back to the bed, and sat down, thinking over what he had told her. It all sounded so ridiculous out loud, but Bob knew in his heart that he was right, that you can buck the police, you can buck the government, and in some cases people have gotten away with bucking armies that outnumber them a hundred to one, but you can't buck the dark forces that lie hidden beneath the surface, the ones some people call luck and others call fate, the ones that decide day after day who will live and who will die, who will win and who will lose.

Bob got to work late the next morning because he didn't have a clock or anyone to get him up. When he entered the shop, Clarence was waiting for him. "Well, did you get the old feller to the doctor on time this morning as well?"

"I don't suppose you would believe me if I told you that I don't have an alarm clock and can't afford to buy one, would you?" Bob said.

"Okay, buster," Clarence came back. "When we get off work tonight you come along with me and I'll take

you downtown and buy you a clock, if that's all it will take
to get you to work on time. I just hope you don't think
you can keep on clinging to your old jailhouse habits
here on the job, though. You got to move, man, drill
them holes, unlock those jigs. We're a production shop.
You walk around all day like you're in a dream with some
big beautiful broad. This here's a machine shop, man, it
ain't no stage. I suppose you really ain't got no clothes
other than them suits and such to wear to work?''

Bob held out his hands and stalled while thinking up
something to say.

"Don't worry about it. We'll just drop on over to the
Goodwill store and buy you a few work clothes as well.
They won't cost much and you can pay me back as soon
as you get rolling.''

Bob looked surprised. "The Goodwill store?''

"Yeah, the Goodwill store. Don't tell me you're an
American working man and don't know about the Goodwill store. Jesus, you either got to be a commie spy or was
locked up in some jail so long you don't know down from
up.''

Bob grinned and shook his head while heading off to
do his assigned work. Clarence watched the retreating
figure and beamed as if he were watching his only child
just become president of the United States.

That night Clarence took Bob to a store and bought
him an alarm clock. Then they went to Goodwill and Bob
picked out a few pairs of work pants, some work shirts,
and a pair of high-top shoes. All were partially worn and
Bob tried not to hold his nose in the air, but it was
obviously hard for him. Clarence noticed this and muttered, "Yeah, it does take some getting used to. But hell,

everyone does it. Even the rich come to haunt these places nowadays, what with prices the way they are. Where you been, Bob? You weren't really in prison at all, were you? I mean, I was just joshing you about all that, just seeing if you could take it."

Bob smiled at the little old lead man and his concern, and responded, "I was in a different world, Clarence. A planet kind of like this one, but so different in some ways that I don't know if I'll ever get used to this or not."

Clarence looked at Bob oddly, then went back to beaming. "You'll do all right, kid. You're going to make a hell of a driller and as long as you can get to work, you ain't going to get into any trouble there. You won't have time to."

Clarence drove Bob home. When they pulled up in front of the hotel, Clarence shuddered. "Well, you ain't no rich bastard just down at our shop slumming," he said. "I'd considered that too. How do you live in a dump like that? Jesus, no wonder you don't have a clock or no clothes. As big as the rats must be in that joint, they'd probably pack off little items like that."

"Oh, it ain't all that bad," Bob said, smiling. "At least the elevator works. I'll see you tomorrow, Clarence, and I'll be on time—that is, if your clock works."

Bob took the elevator to his floor and looked up and down the hall. When he was certain no one was around, he eased open the utility closet door and stepped inside. He put down his packages and began digging under a pile of rags in one corner. Soon he came up with the package Diane had left him the night before. Then he gathered up all of his packages and took the stairs to the next floor to see Tom. He had to wait again for Tom to

come to the door, and as he stood there, he idly thought
of taking his clothes to his room. But he decided to wait
as he heard Tom struggling around inside, trying to get
to the door. Finally Tom got it open and welcomed Bob
as if he were the last friend left in the world.

"Goddamn, Bob. Tomorrow I'll get up and unlock the
door around five o'clock so that when you come you
won't have to stand out there waiting on me."

"No, that's all right, Tom. You keep your door locked
like always, especially after I give you what I'm going to
give you now."

And then Bob handed over Diane's gift. He didn't
know exactly what was in it, but he had enough confidence in Diane and even Rick to know that if they sent
him something out of the goodness of their hearts, that it
would be extravagant indeed. And it was. The package
held a bottle of a hundred one-sixteenths of Dilaudid
and a bottle of five hundred fifteen-milligram Desoxyn
tablets.

Old Tom whistled. "Jesus Christ, Bob. Where in hell
did you get this?"

Bob shrugged. "Oh, some friends dropped by last
night and left it with me as a going-away present."

Tom whistled again. "Jesus, some friends. I wish I had
friends like that. You know what this little old package is
worth?"

"Yeah, about two thousand dollars, more or less, depending on whether you sell it piecemeal or by the tab. If
you sold it by the tablet, it would run closer to three. And
you do have friends like that, Tom, you got me. Because
I'm giving the package to you. It's yours, no questions
asked. Shoot it up, sell it, or give it away. Makes no

difference to me. It's yours. The only thing is, I was
thinking that this would more than supply your three
dirty urines and would get that out of the way so you
could get on your methadone."

Old Tom looked at Bob suspiciously. "How come
you're doing all this for me? What you got in mind,
Bob?"

"Jesus, you're a suspicious old coot," laughed Bob.
"I'm doing it for you because you're good people. There
ain't many around like you no more, Tom, not many.
And think of all the stuff you gave away when you was fat.
Think back. Didn't you give away a lot of stuff to people
that was hurting? Hell, I remember when we was up in
the joint together and Sally was running for you. You
gave away a lot of stuff then. You even gave some to me a
time or two."

"Is that right, Bob? You know, I can't even remember.
Yeah, I guess I did give away a lot of stuff. But I had it to
give. Obviously, you don't have much or you wouldn't be
stuck off down here in this dingy hotel with me."

Bob laughed again. "Shit, I don't got to stay here,
Tom. I got money, I got anything I want. I just stay here
because I like the company. You go ahead on and knock
your lights out, old thing. I'm going on down to my room
to change clothes and then I'll come back and take you
out to get some chow, or I'll go out and find one of those
chicken joints and get a sackful."

"Ain't you going to try none of this stuff?" Tom asked.
"To hell with chow. We got good dope, man."

Bob turned to leave. "I told you that was yours, old
thing. I got my own stash and you ain't getting to it, so
don't even ask what's in it."

And then Bob strode lightly down the hall and down
the stairs. He placed his parcels on the floor and unlocked his door, then picked up his stuff, entered, and
tossed the packages on the bed. When he opened the
closet to hang up his coat, however, he found himself
face-to-face with a .22-caliber pistol, held by a shaky
hand. The voice behind the gun ordered, "Turn around
slowly and lay facedown on the floor."

Bob hesitated, his mind racing, searching for a way
out. He couldn't come up with anything so he turned
slowly and did as he was told. Now a second figure approached and rummaged through the clothes Bob had
tossed on the bed.

He must have been hiding behind the bed, Bob
thought. He glanced up out of the corner of his eye and
noticed that both assailants wore ski masks. Well, perhaps they didn't intend to kill him, or else they wouldn't
have gone to all that trouble to disguise themselves, Bob
figured.

And then one of the pair kicked Bob in the head.

"Where's it at, Bob, where's it at?"

At first the roaring in Bob's head was so loud he
couldn't make out what the guy had said. When he did
sort out the question, he answered with, "I don't know
what you're talking about. What do you want?"

"We want your dope, man, where's the dope?"

Bob squirmed on the floor as his mind raced. He could
send them up to the old man's room, they might be
satisfied with that and go away. But hell, just losing that
stuff after getting it would probably kill old Tom, not to
mention what this pair might do to him trying to make
him come up with more. Finally Bob said, "Man, I ain't

got no dope. You think I'd be living in this flea trap if I had any dope? Hell, I'm on the methadone program, withdrawing because I couldn't keep up my habit, and you guys come to me to rob me for dope. Boy, that sure is a laugh."

And then Bob tried to laugh to make his point, but it didn't come out right. It sounded more like a howl.

"Okay, buster," one of the pair said. "You want it the hard way, we're just the dudes that can give it to you."

Bob recognized the voice. It was that little punk, David. A picture formed in his mind: the room, Diane, Rick, Nadine, and David, and he, Bob, playing the big-shot role and conning David out of ten grams of speed. He could remember every word said in that room and what he had been thinking, as they now tied his hands to his feet and tied a pillowcase over his head.

"David, you little punk," Bob struggled to say, "I'm telling you the truth. I'm going straight. You ought to try it sometime. It's good for the soul."

"Fucking liar. Where is it, Bob? We know this is all a scam you're playing."

They then began to kick him, and no matter how he squirmed around on the floor he couldn't get away. One of the masked intruders kept kicking him in the side of the head, and each time, blinding streaks of pain exploded in Bob's brain.

The other intruder was bigger and wore pointed-toed cowboy boots. He kept aiming for Bob's ribs. Some of his blows found their way home and some were deflected by Bob's moving shoulders and arms. One caught Bob right at the point of his elbow. His whole arm exploded in a flash of nervous excitement. Yet somehow Bob still seemed to have the presence of mind to reflect on the irony of it all, of all the times that he had lied to bastards like David and then come out on top, and now, when he was actually telling the truth he was getting the shit kicked out of him.

The two masked gunmen kept kicking Bob and then leaning over him, panting and huskily grunting, "Where is it, Bob, where is it?"

Just like on TV, Bob thought, the fucking TV babies. What was the world coming to with all these TV babies? What were the people going to do once they realized that they had raised a whole new breed of little monsters, who were so tuned in to the tube that they looked nowhere else for advice and mental stimulation? What did people on the tube do when they ran across others who were obvious obstacles in their life? They shot or stabbed them, or ran over them with a truck.

The sad part was, it was all so stupid, thought Bob. Who would ever go to a fleabag hotel to rob a mark? Nobody but a stupid TV baby, some lump kid who'd been raised on nothing but animal crackers and cold breakfast cereal every day of his immature life.

And right then for some reason, Bob picked up a flash of inspiration. He knew he was about to die. It just came to him and he knew it. He thought about how stupid it was to die in this manner. How stupid and mad could they get? Bob relaxed and quit trying to fend off the continual rain of blows. It hadn't seemed to help anyway, and now he only felt the occasional one that really came on through and rocked his whole being.

Hell, he told himself, I should have stayed on the road. I was really dumb to think that the hat would not come and get me. I should have realized that cleaning up my hand wouldn't make any difference to the hat. And poor Diane, what's to become of her? She looked so damn good last night too. I just wish now that I had wrassled her on down and proceeded to do everything she had been crying for for so long. She might even have stayed with me, or better yet, she might have drug me off.

Finally the attackers ran completely out of breath. They stood there wondering if Bob was still conscious. Then David asked his companion, "What are we going to do? The bastard either doesn't have it or he's going to die before he tells us where it's at."

"Kill the sonofabitch. I'll bet you then that the next bastard we capture will tell us where it is at. So, he's tough. They ain't all going to be tough. I say, kill him."

David raised his .22-caliber pistol and shot Bob twice in the back. The little gun made a lot of noise in the closed room. It made enough for the old lady next door, who by then had placed her ear up against the wall.

As soon as she heard the two intruders leave, she headed for the phone in the lobby and called the police.

Detective Gentry was just stepping out of his office when an officer from the dispatch center ran up. "They just picked up that Bob Hughes over in the old Atmore Hotel. He's been badly beaten and has two gunshot wounds."

Gentry closed his eyes and muttered, "Oh no, oh goddamn, that stupid sonofabitch."

Gentry raced out of the stationhouse and down the street to his parked car. It took him only minutes to cross the central district of downtown Portland, and then find the old Atmore Hotel down on Burnside Street. An ambulance was already there, and in the drizzling rain its revolving red and blue lights were casting eerie patterns on the street and buildings. Police cars were also pulled up to the scene. Gentry parked between two of the other patrol cars and hurried to the side of a white-draped stretcher bringing Bob out of the hotel. No blanket covered Bob's face, so Gentry figured he wasn't dead. How could that lump Halamer be so dumb as to beat and shoot someone and then let them live to tell about it?

Gentry pushed his way into the back of the ambulance along with Bob and the ambulance attendant. One look at Bob's pasty-white features convinced Gentry that Bob's condition was poor. Bob was having a tough time focusing his eyes and seemed unaware of where he was or what was transpiring. He didn't look good at all.

"How's he doing?" Gentry asked the attendant.

The nurse looked up at Gentry, hesitated, and gave the thumbs-down gesture.

Gentry squatted down in the moving ambulance and gripped Bob's hand. "You awake, Bob? You okay?"

Bob strained and tried to refocus his eyes. He saw who Gentry was and smiled through the blood that frothed around his lips.

"Who got you, Bob? Was it your old antagonist, my friend?" Gentry was afraid to ask Bob directly if it had been Halamer who had shot him, with the attendant as a witness hovering close by.

Bob seemed to understand even that in a moment of lucidity, and he smiled more as he shook his head. Just briefly Bob considered saying, yes, it was the tough cop he hated so much, but then he reconsidered. He'd never been a rat in his whole life. Why go out as one now?

Relief flooded through Gentry and he relaxed as he swayed back and forth with the ambulance's erratic motions. "Who shot you, Bob? What happened?"

Bob then choked out, "The hat."

Gentry leaned down closer to Bob's lips. "The hat, Bob? Did you say the hat?"

Bob almost lifted his head off the ambulance's pillow as he impatiently tried to nod. "Tell Diane to watch out for the hat, the hat's going to get her too. Tell—"

"Okay, I'll tell Diane to watch out for the hat. Did the hat shoot you, Bob?"

Bob's mind drifted in and out of consciousness. The last few months of his life seemed to pass unhurriedly before him. He watched Nadine ask for a puppy to hold and pet, watched his mother condemn him for being what he was, what he'd always been. He held Diane through the many long nights when neither of them could sleep.

Then he came out of his languid dream world and the interior lights of the ambulance began to brighten. He saw Gentry again. Gentry kept asking, as though it was very important, "Was it the hat that shot you, Bob?"

"No, the TV baby shot me."

"The TV baby shot you, but the hat sent him, is that right?"

Bob nodded again. Blood completely filled his mouth

now and he couldn't speak, he could only try to cough. And the light, the light was so bright now, ever so bright.

Bob Hughes arrived at Memorial Hospital in downtown Portland, Oregon, at seven twenty-one P.M. and was pronounced dead on arrival.

Printed in the United States
by Baker & Taylor Publisher Services